The Clear Blue Line

Also by Al Sprague

*The Mahogany Tree * El árbol de caoba*
*Windswept * Vendaval*

The
CLEAR
BLUE
LINE

a novel　　　　AL SPRAGUE

BACON PRESS
BOOKS

Washington, D.C.

Published in the United States by Bacon Press Books, Washington, DC
www.baconpressbooks.com

Editor and Copyeditor: Lorraine Fico-White
www.magnificomanuscripts.com

Cover Design and Book Layout and Map Design: Alan Pranke
www.amp13.com

Cover Painting:
Al Sprague

Author Photo:
Brian La Barr

ISBN: 978-0-9913443-1-4
Library of Congress Control Number: 2014942881

PRINTED IN THE UNITED STATES OF AMERICA

I dedicate this book to Jerry Coffey,
the greatest diver I have ever known.

The Clear Blue Line

PREFACE

I had to write this book. The twenty-five years I spent free diving (diving with just the air in one's lungs) were the wildest part of my life. My friends and I were quite mad. We drank too much, fought, and chased women. We ran amuck.

Like free diving, the mysterious sport of spearfishing was a cult that required blind faith and total commitment. The excitement of the hunt was absolutely thrilling. We could almost touch our quarry. The gun clacked, and we struggled with our fish beneath tons of water with nowhere to breathe. Many times a diver would be caught in a strong current, a mile from land and unable to see the bottom. Just one drop of water down the wrong tube at the wrong time and you drowned, immersed in all that killing fluid.

Diving was a macho game back then. We always showed off for the girls. Peer pressure made us take chances. If someone tweaked the tail of a big tiger shark, then the next week someone else would upstage him by dropping in the water behind a working shrimp boat to be swarmed by sharks. From timid novices to bold invaders of the oceans, all of us dove sober and drunk, with a recklessness that should have been our demise.

I don't know how we survived years of diving. What were we looking for? I don't really know, except maybe to be somebody who could stand up and say, "Look at me! Look what I did!"

I've lived an adventurous life, filled with dangerous events, big fish, and colorful personalities. Come with me as we reenter some of my hazardous journeys. While I have participated in or witnessed many of the events in this book (with the grateful exception of killing), it is a mostly fictitious tale. Together, we will explore the liquid blue of the Panama Pacific, where the worst sharks are not always found in the ocean.

Al Sprague
Balboa Yacht Club, Panama
December 21, 2013

COSTA
RICA

CARIBBEAN

PANAMA

PEARL
ISLANDS

PACIFIC

OCEAN

COLOMBIA

Isla Pacheca

Isla Saboga   Isla Contadora

Isla Chitré   Isla Chapera
               Isla Mogo Mogo
Isla Bolaños
Isla Gibraleón   Isla Casayeta
                 Isla Casaya
Isla Bayoneta   Isla La Mina

Isla Señora   Isla
               Viveros   SAN MIGUEL

                                   Isla Cañas
               Isla del Rey
Isla Pedro   ENSENADA   Isla
González   de Puerco

                          Isla San Telmo
        Isla
        San José   Isla Galera

CHAPTER ONE

Every night he returned to Panama in his dreams. Those beautiful islands and friends long vanished returned to the stage, fresh and vital, ready to perform in the play of youth, stamina, and danger. While four decades had passed, Jack Savage knew he would drift through the Pearl Islands for the rest of his life. He remembered the poem, "Up by ten, down by noon, three o'clock, rough water soon," the formula for the dry season wind and weather from the end of December to mid-March. Cold water, upwelling, and fish—big ones and plenty of them. He never could resist the thrill of the chase, no matter how dangerous.

Once again, Jack could feel the three o'clock wind and see the whitecaps churning toward Pacheca Island. He was on his boat, slowly emerging from the camouflage of the foaming surface. It flew across the waves, pounding up and down with such force that the occupants bounced around like tap dancers. It was another three-day trip to the Pearl Islands. carried out with complete abandon.

Young and fearless, Jack steered the boat and steadied himself with the wheel. His good friend, Paul Delsey, held onto the left side of the boat and part of the windshield. In the center, Nick Barber, otherwise known as The Great Spearing Dude, had very little to grasp, except the top of the windshield. He occasionally grabbed at his shipmates, but they shrugged him off. They tried to drink beer out of cans as they lurched through the maelstrom. The Dude talked excitedly as he drank and spilled beer foam. He slipped, was lifted into the air, and then was slammed back to the deck. He swallowed mouthfuls of cold, green seawater that cascaded onto his laughing face.

The boat was full of gas cans, dive gear, flippers, masks, snorkels, wet suits, spearguns, clothing, and personal items in constant motion and complete disarray on the small deck. Nothing could be wetter, and no one could be more beat-up than the three friends of the little *Toulouse* as it sped past the Isle of Pachequilla and into the lee of Saboga, Pacheca, Contadora, and the north end of the Pearl Islands. The forty-mile trip was a classic case study in masochism and stupidity. The small, open boat had earned its title of "ship of fools."

Radio, life jackets, and any other emergency equipment had been removed to make more room for beer, the elixir of life from breakfast to supper. Gasoline was stored in everything from regular gas cans to Clorox bottles. Safety never crossed their minds. They used a Girl Scout compass and memorized numbers to navigate. Eating wasn't a priority. The only food aboard was canned sardines and Vienna sausages. If they got too hungry, they could always take a piece of fish to shore and cook it over some burning driftwood, if they could stand the mosquitoes and sand fleas.

The ocean water during dry season was a brownish-green with a visibility of about thirty feet on a good day to about three feet on a bad day. It was cold, so cold that a wet suit top was necessary. Using a snorkel was as far as they'd go for air. Free divers didn't use anything but the air in their lungs.

Jack stopped the boat in the lee of Pacheca Island. It was his boat, and he dove first. He entered the water wearing his wet suit, dive mask, snorkel, and flippers. He held his speargun in his right hand. The cold shock of the water took his breath away. Beyond the surface, it immediately became colder until the upwelling from the bottom stopped him like a brick wall. His body hung, suspended in the frigid green liquid while huge fish came out of the gloom. It all looked too perfect, and Jack had an uneasy feeling about diving here, but he did it anyway.

Out of the left corner of his eye, he spotted three luminous shapes. As they lazily approached, he saw three large amberjack coming closer and closer until they turned their glowing bodies to the side. Jack extended his arm and pulled the trigger. A spear shaft darted through one of the amberjack. For a moment, the big fish hesitated. It looked like a kill shot. When Jack pulled in the line and the detachable spearpoint slammed crosswise into the fish, the amberjack shook its head and dashed off with all the speed and strength of its powerful body. Down it plunged, twisting, spinning, in complete panic, no longer in control. The animal was at its wildest, fighting for its life. Jack held onto his gun while being dragged behind it into the cold, dark depths. He bit down hard on his snorkel's mouthpiece, but even that was torn away in the viscous wash. When Jack's breath was almost gone, he pulled the release lever on his Riffe reel and headed toward the surface.

He cleared the water in a violent splash, gasping for air and shaking his gun to let the men in the boat see the loose rubbers of the speargun indicating he had a fish. In an instant, he was plunged down into the depths again, struggling with the big fish as it dove deeper, thirty, forty, fifty feet. Jack's ears were bursting. He needed air badly, but he doggedly hung onto his gun. Vertigo hit him in flashes. Up or down made no difference. The cold water and depth had disrupted his sense of balance.

Finally Jack pulled the release lever the second time and headed for the surface, his flippers a blur, praying he had enough line left to reach air for his burning lungs. He tore through the liquid ceiling, kicking and pulling up on the line desperately. The fish powered Jack through the surface with enough of his face out of the water to gasp an occasional breath of air. He choked, but free divers knew how to choke and still breathe spray. The men in the boat were speeding over to him. Jack struggled to keep his head out of the water. Three feet from the boat, he was pulled down a third time.

He was exhausted. He mustered all his strength and with one last effort, kicked his legs. He stretched his body and whipped his neck back until his vertebrae crackled. He blasted through the water next to the boat and welcome hands grabbed his gun. Jack could barely pull himself into the boat. He slid down onto the deck, thoroughly wasted. Paul and the Dude yanked the fighting amberjack into the boat and sent it flopping all over Jack, covering him with fish slime and blood.

"Get that damn fish off of me!" he yelled, then vomited.

Night came quickly as it always did in the tropics. At six o'clock, darkness pounced. The three divers filleted their fish, packed the chunks into plastic bags, and placed the bags in the Igloo cooler. A can of Vienna sausages and one of sardines was passed around for supper.

"Woulda been nice with some crackers. Who the hell was in charge of provisioning this tub?" the Dude grumbled.

"You think crackers would've survived the beating we got today? Next time do your own shopping," Paul said out of the darkness.

"Ah, you guys're always bitching. Find a nice fish head for a pillow and go to sleep," Jack said.

"Sleep? Did the man say sleep? Not for The Great Spearing Dude. Ain't nobody gonna sleep at nine o'clock at night! I'm just beginning to wake up. I'm takin' my fish head an' I'm gonna catch me a big shark. Yessiree, I'm gonna pull a two-thousand-pound tiger shark into this boat, green as hell, snappin' an' snarlin', an' if you're sleepin', he's gonna bite your ass off."

"That'll be the day," Jack said.

"Hey, don't bait the bastard," Paul said and laughed. "Let him babble on or we'll be up all night."

"We'll see. Just wait'n see what's comin' into this boat to sandpaper your asses," the Dude said.

"Asshole," the other two murmured as they laid their heads on the slimy deck.

There was a clinking of chain, as the Dude baited the shark hook with a big fish carcass. A whir of a heavy line sounded as he swung the baited hook overhead, followed by a splash in the water and the sound of tying rope on a cleat. After the ripples from the splash stopped slapping the side of the boat, there was silence.

The familiar north wind howled through the trees on the top of Contadora Island. It was nice to be on the boat in the lee of the island and out of the way of the beastly wind, Jack thought. Occasionally, the croak of a pelican burped out from the jungle trees. Bats swooped close enough for Jack to hear their wings flutter, snatching insects from the dark. The stars were magnificent. Not a cloud in the sky. The Dippers, the Southern Cross, they were all there as the main attraction. Earth was the floater. The sensation of vastness and eternity overwhelmed him. The secret of life was out there—peace at its utmost. The soothing, natural silence lulled Jack to sleep.

He woke to a rasping sound as the Dude's shark line scraped over the cramped deck of the *Toulouse*. The line dragged through the tangled mass of people and equipment to the stern.

"What th—"

The thick shark line stopped at the tie-off cleat, swinging the whole boat around from its anchor. Everyone jumped up, then stumbled and slid all over the deck. Fish slime, dive gear, spearpoints, the cooler, and bodies were booby traps in the dark. There wouldn't be any light until sunup, as no one had thought to bring a flashlight. The closest thing to illumination, save the stars, was phosphorescence from miniscule sea-life in the ocean as the shark line sliced through the water and the boat moved backward quickly.

"What the hell's on that fuckin' line?" Jack yelled. A ghostly glow, longer than the boat and almost as wide, surfaced not far from them. "It's a tiger shark!"

"Told you guys I'd get something big on there," the Dude said.

"You idiot! We're taking water over the stern. We're going down ass first unless we get it off the line. The anchor's dragging in the sand."

Water cascaded over the transom in sheets.

"Find a bucket. Let's get bailing!" Paul shouted.

Jack fumbled for a bucket and began to bail. The Dude held the line and tried to pull the monster up to the side. Jack bailed frantically as the small boat took on more water with each jerk of the shark line.

Paul yelled to the Dude. "Find a knife or something! This is no time to go fishing. Get a hold of something sharp. Cut him off before he sinks us."

"I found one. I found one. You sure you want me to cut the line? Sure you don't want to catch it to see what it is?"

"You want to go swimming with it? Give me the knife." Paul yanked it out of the Dude's hand and shoved him out of the way. He felt his way over to the cleat, found the stretched rope, and slashed at it. The line snapped and sounded like the crack of a gunshot. The backlashing line smacked Paul across his cheekbone.

"You lost my shark," the Dude said. "It coulda' been a record."

"Chucha," Paul said. "We almost sink and go swimming with a monster shark and you're griping about not catching it? Dude, you ain't got the brains of a mackerel. Get a damn fish head and go to sleep."

"Ain't got no fish head. Shark ate it."

"Tough," Jack said. "Looks like you don't have a pillow for the night. You're just going to have to sleep on the deck. Now go to sleep."

The Dude laid down and muttered himself to sleep.

The mango-red globe of the sun that seemed to ooze from the Pacific followed the light of dawn. Jack woke with a yawn and pried himself from the sticky, fish deck. He rose to his feet with some effort and tried to stretch the pain out of his beat-up body. Paul was already up, taking a leak over the side.

"That moron." Jack shook his head, looking at the Dude's crumpled shape under the transom.

"We ought to throw his worthless ass overboard," Paul said.

"Do you want to?"

"Yeah, let's do it. The water's about sixty-eight degrees. It'll wake him up quick."

Both men grabbed the slumbering Dude. Before he could wake up, he was airborne. He hit the water with a tremendous splash and then disappeared. He wasn't out of the picture for long. He blasted out of the frigid water, sucking air in loud gasping sounds.

"Sonofabitch!" he said, heaving himself back onto the boat. "What the hell was that for?"

"Last night."

"Y'know, the shark."

"Fuck you. That cold water almost stopped my heart."

"We couldn't be so lucky," Paul said.

"Yeah, Dude. After you wiped out the boat and almost sank us with that idiotic shark stunt of yours, then drank half of our beer to get to sleep, you definitely had it coming," Jack said.

"I'll tell you what. Tonight I'm gonna slipknot the shark line to the both of you an' you're goin' in."

"I swear to God, Dude, you go shark fishing again and I'll shoot you with my speargun," Paul said.

"That makes two of us," Jack said.

"Asses. Nothin' but masses of asses," the Dude said quietly.

"Hey, Dude," Jack said. "Don't get pissed off . . . just get off."

Paul tried to hide his laughter.

The Great Spearing Dude fumed. Jack and Paul knew he was a classic pig, but that's why they liked him. He was a likeable pig. They had been diving with the Dude for years, and he hadn't changed a bit—impulsive, crazy, and always out for adventure.

"C'mon, Dude. Lighten up. It was all in fun." Jack grabbed him around the neck and tried to shake him.

"Yeah, fun for you."

"C'mon, c'mon," Paul said. "You can get even with us later. Let's go diving. We didn't come here to gripe."

The Dude smiled and said, "Ah, why not."

They agreed to go to some distant dive spots down the island chain. To be safe, Jack decided to hide two large cans of gasoline on Pacheca Island to lighten the boat. They would pick up the cans on the way back for their homebound gasoline.

Jack knew the jungle almost as well as he knew the ocean. He set the cans in an out-of-the-way spot, far from any trails, and concealed them with roots and leaves. He made sure the red of the cans was completely camouflaged. Then they took off for an island twenty miles away.

By the time they reached Elefante, they had nearly polished off a case of beer. They hit the island at the right time. Giant jewfish lay motionless on the shallower sandy ledge. Broomtail grouper, dogtooth cubera snapper, and the special, sought after prize, the silver corbina, lined the rocky bottom, waiting for the drift to bring baitfish to them.

The water was a cold, clear green with visibility about thirty feet. Things couldn't have been better for the divers. Their method of diving had two men in the water and one man in the boat. The engine always purred in neutral, ready to go. The driver focused on the divers and the boat's proximity to the rocks. The divers looked out for each other and the fish.

All three of them could make sixty-foot dives and stay down two minutes, if necessary. Paul was an exception. He could free dive one hundred feet and stay down five minutes. He had earned the title of "best and most famous diver in Panama."

Paul and the Dude were in the water with Jack as the driver. Jack eyed the Dude's snorkel and mentally marked the area where he had disappeared beneath the surface. Paul didn't use a snorkel. He put his head out of the water, gulped air, and slid down flipper first until he was well underwater, then pointed toward the bottom and glided away, never making so much as a ripple. His whole movement was as graceful as a ballerina's.

Crimson snapper, ten to twenty pounds, swarmed over the surface and clustered around the divers like moths around a light bulb. The snapper glowed fluorescent red, like big goldfish. Hefty, sixty-pound amberjack crowded in to look at the curious forms of the intruders.

Jack wanted one of them to get a fish quickly so he could get in. He saw Paul's head break the surface not far from the Dude.

"Lots of corbina down there. About fifty, sixty feet."

One big breath and Paul disappeared again. He easily moved his flippers back and forth, like a man walking upside down in slow motion. His light skin glowed for a while, then disappeared into the murk.

A long moment later, Paul's head broke the surface again. He struggled with a fish and raised his gun so Jack could see it. Jack raced to the spot. He grabbed the heavy tuna line attached to the spear and began pulling in the fish as Paul slid into the boat. Paul took back the line, and a big, silver corbina flew into the boat. Paul knelt down to remove the detachable spearpoint. The fish slapped its tail vigorously, splattering Paul with blood.

"It's a beauty," Jack said. "What do you think it weighs?"

"About twenty-five, thirty pounds."

"Good fish."

"There's plenty more down there. Go get one. It's a bitch current so stay close to the rocks."

"Any sharks?"

"Nah, just those shitty, annoying little whitetips."

Jack gave Paul the wheel and slid over the side. He kept close to the rock wall of the island, using the eddy to work himself upstream and to keep in neutral motion while he prepared to dive. He heard the clack of the Dude's speargun when it went off somewhere in the depths. The Great Spearing Dude never missed. There were more metallic clanking sounds after the shot. They seemed to pass right under him and head out to sea.

Jack took a great breath and launched his body downward. He had to pinch his nose when he descended to clear his ears. It was cold and dark. Everything was an olive haze. Finally, the light reflecting off the sand bottom hit his eyes. He was deep, deeper than he normally dove. He hung there, suspended in the gloom, and let the current take his body. Suddenly, a huge, silvery mass loomed in front of him. He drifted toward it, as if he were frozen. Jack knew if he moved so much as a finger the whole school of corbina would be gone in one communal clap of gills. As he approached the school, he moved his speargun up slowly, like a floating part of his body. He held the pistol grip with one hand and extended the gun outward toward the fish. His movements mimicked the current, like a piece of debris flowing along in slow motion.

To shoot corbina, he had to move in close, shoot the nearest one without hesitation, and shoot it through the middle. Otherwise the spearpoint would pull out of the soft flesh. His gun clacked when he launched the rubber-powered spear. It tore through a fish. The entire school vanished instantly. Jack had nailed a big one. It pulled hard but didn't compare to an amberjack.

On his way to the surface, Jack had to give a little line. He felt the urge to breathe. He had been down longer than he realized. The closer he got to the surface, the more lightheaded he became. Finally, he could see the cellophane ripple of the top above him. He knew he was in the first stages of shallow water blackout. He'd known divers who'd lost consciousness about three feet from the surface. It was caused by the buildup of carbon dioxide in the brain that expanded as a diver came up.

Jack swallowed again and again, fighting the urge to breathe. He blinked his eyes rapidly, squeezing his lids together tightly. He tried to erase the black dots and white flashes that danced across his vision. He held on and thrust through the watery barrier into delicious air. He gulped at it greedily.

"Looks like you beat me," Paul said as Jack pulled in a huge corbina. "Have you seen the Dude?"

"No, why?"

"I haven't seen hide nor hair of him since before you went down."

"I heard him shoot and then heard a lot of metallic clanking sounds beneath me, heading out to sea. I didn't think much of it because you know his capability for the bizarre."

"I'll bet the dumb bastard's lost his gun. That clanking sound was probably his gun bouncing over the rocks with a huge jewfish on the other end of it. I just hope to God he wasn't attached to it. *Puta.* We've got our work cut out for us. You said that the clanking sound headed out to deep water?"

"Yeah."

"Okay, with the time that's elapsed since you went down, and the direction you said you thought the sound traveled, and the speed of the current, I'd say we'd better head out this way."

Paul wheeled the boat around and cruised at a moderate speed, looking with eagle-eye precision. Jack scanned the surface.

"Sonofabitch! He's always fucking up . . . always." Jack was more upset than mad. The Great Spearing Dude was like a brother to him. The thought of him drowning gave Jack the chills.

Paul searched the ocean like a hungry frigate bird. "We'll find him. We've got to find him. I hope that jewfish hasn't tangled him up and the sharks aren't munching his ass."

They motored and drifted back and forth for more than an hour, covering at least two or three miles of ocean. Finally, Paul and Jack looked at each other despondently.

"I don't know, Jack. Looks like he might be gone."

"We could organize a search party for him." Jack was close to tears, but he'd never let Paul know it.

"Might as well head back to Elefante. Who knows?" Paul pushed the throttle down.

They traveled back to the island slowly, against wind and current, still looking for the Dude. The mood was grim. About two miles from Elefante, Paul spotted something in the distance. "Hey, look over there on that big, floating banana tree. Over there. Is that a bird? What's that flopping around in the water . . . or on it?"

"What? Where?"

"Over there." Paul turned the boat in the direction of the floating debris.

"Chucha. It's something . . . something alive."

"It ain't no bird." Paul laughed. "It's an asshole."

"Oh, God," Jack said. "Oh, thank God."

They pulled up to a floating hulk of a banana tree connected to a wild-eyed Nick Barber. Paul didn't pick him up right away but circled him.

"Hey, lemme in the boat! I've been kickin' sharks for an hour! They're still under me."

"They aren't going to bite you. Did you shoot a big jewfish in the tail?"

"Yes. Yes. Now lemme in the boat!"

Paul and Jack pulled in the exhausted, shivering Dude.

"Cover him up," Jack said. "He's freezing his ass off. If he goes into shock, we'll be bringing a stiff back with all this fish."

Both men covered the Dude with anything they could find. Fortunately, he still had his wet suit on. Paul gunned the engine for a rough ride back to Pacheca.

"Damn, Jack, he's in bad shape."

"You handle the steering; I'll keep him alive."

Jack pulled a small flask of gin from his bag. "Nick, can you take a sip of this?"

The Dude's shaking worsened, but he nodded his head for a sip. After a few more nips, he settled down.

"I feel better."

"Geez, you were shaking worse than a dog trying to shit a peach seed."

The Dude appeared to be asleep but Jack checked his pulse . . . just in case.

CHAPTER TWO

"**D**amnit!" Jack shouted. They had retraced their steps through the jungle on Pacheca Island.

"What?" The Dude came running.

"The natives stole our gas."

"Oh, maan, no."

"How did the bastards find it?" Paul shook his head.

"They must have been watching us when we went ashore to hide the cans." Jack kicked a tree in frustration. "It's another ball game now."

They searched the area again, but the cans were definitely gone. They swam back out to the boat to consider their options.

"We could go over to Saboga Island and shoot up the village until someone comes forward with the gas. Hell, I've been wanting to try out that ol' sawed off Mossberg shotgun for a long time." The Dude rubbed his hands together.

"Nah, the Guardia would get us in no time. Anyway, we don't even know if it was anyone from Saboga. It could even be some thieves from the town of San Miguel on Rey Island or Mafafa or Pedro Gonzales or some passing fishermen that saw us carry the gas onto the island," Jack said. "Funny thing is most people around here are honest."

"Well, we gotta think of something," Paul said. "We can't go home on fumes."

"How 'bout if we add fifty percent seawater to the gas? That'll fill the tanks and we can get home half as fast," the Dude said.

"You're a moron, y'know." Paul looked like he was getting ready to swat him. The Dude chuckled.

"I think I've got an idea," Jack said. "Why don't we jiggle all the containers around to see how much gas is in them, then pour every little drop into a few cans. We just might have enough gas to get home, or close to it."

"Don't think we have any other choice," Paul said.

"We better get at it before that damn wind comes up, or we'll never make it." Jack picked up the near-empty gas can.

After they'd rounded up every type of container they had used for gasoline and emptied them into the two standard gas cans, they had just under twelve gallons, nearly two tankfuls.

"I don't know, man." Jack chewed on his lower lip. "That doesn't look like a helluva lotta gas for our trip home."

"Let's say we make three miles to the gallon. That's if the wind doesn't come up. Hell, that's almost thirty-six miles. We'd probably be in the anchorage or just off Flamenco Island before we crap out. We could paddle in from there," Paul said.

"No paddles," the Dude said.

"We can get out of the boat with our flippers on and kick the damn thing in."

"I'm for it," Jack said.

The Dude nodded. "Count me in. There's no place like home. Even if you don't get there."

"We're gonna have to lighten the boat." Paul looked around. "That means we've got to dump the fish."

"Aww, no."

"Yep, and the Dude goes over, too, halfway back."

"Fuck you, Delsey."

Paul laughed.

"What a waste of life and food," Jack said. He helped dump the contents of the big cooler over the side.

"I don't like killing fish and wasting them either, Jack, but it's our asses that are on the line now." Paul washed off the cooler.

The Dude pulled up the anchor, and Jack started the engine. He had a big lump in his throat as he followed the heading three-zero-five on the plastic, handheld, Girl Scout compass. Jack always had a fear of conking out in the big, empty ocean. The thought of drifting around helplessly almost paralyzed him.

The way back from the Pearl Islands could be idyllic or terrifying. A small boat of fifteen feet was no match for God's great ocean. The skin of the boat's hull was no more than a quarter- to half-inch thickness, small defense against murderous breaking waves that pounded one after the other for miles in a storm.

"Aww shit," the Dude said. "There are whitecaps off Pachequilla. We'll never get up on a plane. There goes our gas."

"There's always whitecaps off Pachequilla. It's the current," Paul said.

When they came out of the lee of Pacheca and rounded the little isle of Pachequilla, crushing, white-capped waves smashed into them. The little boat flew over a few of them, but the beating was too much for fiberglass and human flesh. They had to slow down. The boat wallowed and tossed in the current and tide maelstrom of Panama Bay for more than an hour.

"At this rate we're gonna run out of gas!" Jack shouted above the roar of wave and engine.

"I know this place," Paul said. "It'll calm down more when we get into the big middle. That wind will die down before noon."

There was no land in sight anywhere. The dry season fires on the mainland made for an orange, closed-in void, and visibility wasn't more than a few miles.

Then, just as Paul had predicted, the wind abated.

"Damn Sam! Paul, you were right!" Jack shouted.

Finally, under the furnace of the sun, the choppy surface of the ocean seemed to melt, looking like an orange puddle of molten lead. Jack goosed the engine, and the boat planed on the slick surface of the water. He checked his compass constantly. They had been traveling too long not to see land. The atmosphere was thick with smoke, and the visibility was getting worse.

Paul looked over to Jack. "You keeping a good heading on that *chichipate* compass of yours?"

"Good as I can. I'm sure we're on the mark. Hey, Dude, how much gas we got left?"

The Dude sat on the empty cooler. He looked down at the last tank of gas and cupped his hands to his mouth. "'Bout five gallons. Shit, not much. Sure would like to see some land."

"We will, we will."

Everyone became silent. The lump in Jack's throat nearly choked him. He felt like screaming but didn't want to show any emotion in front of his friends. Paul scanned the horizon, trying to see through the smoke coming off the burning jungle.

The silence continued for thirty minutes until Paul gave a loud shout. "Hey, there's Flamenco Island and the ships in the anchorage. We could paddle in from here."

"Ain't got no paddle." The Dude smiled.

Paul ignored him. "How much gas, Dude?"

"'Bout a gallon and a half, maybe two."

"Come on, *Toulouse*, you can make it. Come on, old boy." Jack pleaded, willing the boat forward.

They passed the last ship in the anchorage waiting to go through the Panama Canal. Eventually "C" buoy, the end marker of the canal, was eclipsed. Suddenly a shabby, black boat appeared, coming down the canal from behind.

"Hey, maybe we don't have to paddle after all," Paul said.

All three divers looked at the boat before waving.

"It's El Gigante's meat barge," the Dude said. "Don't want no help from that bastard."

"Hell, a boat's a boat," Paul said, annoyed.

"Not that one."

"And why not that one?"

"'Cause it's a drug smuggling, killer's boat," Jack said. "Get a ride with him and you'll never return."

Jack kept his eyes straight ahead, looking down the buoys of the canal and avoiding eye contact with the men on the other boat. He remembered the night the Dude and he were down at the Balboa Yacht Club, sipping on a few brews. A big argument had broken out at the end of the bar between three young men who weren't regular customers. One of them was Juan Vergara's son. A good kid in with the wrong crowd. Jack saw the man they called El Gigante nod. Two of his thugs picked up the young man, walked him all the way down the pier and onto the black boat with the poorly running diesel engine. Jack would never forget the scream that was louder than the engine noise. About an hour later, the black boat returned. There were only two men walking down the pier. Juan had sworn he would get even one day. Jack, loyal to his friends beyond reason, promised if he ever got the chance, he'd help Juan get revenge. But right now, he didn't want any more trouble.

"Just ignore them," Jack said.

The shabby black boat passed by.

Ten minutes later, they were almost parallel to Flamenco Island when the old Mercury sped up, coughed, then died of thirst.

"Well, that's it, gents." Jack threw his hands up. "Guess we're out of gas. It's flipper time." They put their flippers on and dropped overboard. Jack and Paul each took a side, and the Dude kicked from behind.

"We are lucky. The tide's going out," the Dude said.

With a ten- to eighteen-foot tide in Panama Bay, the current ran out of the canal like a river.

"Just keep kicking. Maybe we can snag onto a buoy or something," Jack said.

They missed all the buoys and headed out to sea again.

"Let's anchor," the Dude said.

"Not enough anchor line."

"If we miss 'C' buoy," Paul said, "our ass is grass."

They missed it. They climbed back into the boat again and drifted for about an hour in a somber mood. Paul stood up slowly, as if he was going to stretch. He turned to the other two with a sly grin on his face. He kept grinning.

"A boat's coming up behind us."

"*Chucha madre.* A boat? Where? Show me." The Dude tripped over Jack, and they both fell down laughing.

"It's Walter Mendoza," Paul said, breaking into a broad smile.

"Walter's a good guy, but watch out for Rachel, his old lady," the Dude said. "She can rip your balls off in a second. She damn near tore mine off, and I didn't do nothing."

"Yeah, I know, Dude. Perfectly innocent. You probably pinched that gorgeous ass of hers," Jack said.

"*Moi?* Not a chance, but I really would like to. What an ass."

"You guys keep your opinions to yourselves," Paul said.

Paul knew Walter would help them out. Unlikely as it seemed, they had become friends even though they were almost each other's opposite.

Where Paul was muscular and athletic, Walter was round and soft. Paul always struggled for money while Walter lived an easy life, not wanting for anything. But since Paul was considered a national hero as the best diver in Panama, in Walter's eyes, that made them equals. Walter had once told Paul he would do anything for him. He was happy to tie off the *Toulouse* to his boat, the *Rachel Red,* and tow them into the Balboa Yacht Club float.

Jack went to the gas pump and filled one of his six-gallon cans. He noticed Rachel standing off to one side while Paul and Walter were in deep discussion about diving and boats. She was one of the most stunning women Jack had ever seen. Her flaming red hair complimented her slight sunburn and her green eyes. There was something so sensuous and enticing about her lips, Jack couldn't keep himself from staring.

"I'd like to fuck her brains out," the Dude said quietly to Jack. "I'm getting a hard-on so bad that I'm gonna trip and pole vault off this float." He squirmed.

"Forget it," Jack said.

The launch that ferried boat owners to their moorings pulled up to the dock. Two men stepped off the launch, walked up to Walter, and said something to him. The man with the pigtail grabbed Walter and hit him across the face with the back of his fist. Blood poured from Walter's nose. Paul jumped in, but he was a better diver than a fighter and got poled in the mouth by the shorter man. Rachel screamed.

It all happened so fast, it didn't register with Jack right away. "Hey, assholes!" he finally yelled.

The two turned toward Jack and lunged. Jack's bare foot came up so swiftly it was never seen. It caught the shorter one between the legs. The man's eyes crossed, his hands groped his crotch, and he hit the deck with a meaty thud.

The other man swung at Jack and hit his cheekbone with a glancing blow. Jack deftly turned around and grabbed his opponent's pigtail, putting his knee up behind the man's back and pulling backward on the pigtail. He threw him to the deck, landed on him with his knees, and proceeded to beat him until Paul pulled him off.

"I don't like you," Jack said, still angry. "If you see me in the future, leave. If you know I'm gonna be somewhere, don't go, and keep away from my friend, Walter."

Jack threw both of them into the water and turned to Walter. "How you doing?"

"Jack, I can't thank you enough."

"No sweat. That's what friends are for."

"Man, where did you learn to fight like that?" the Dude asked.

"I watched the animals in the jungle, the fish underwater, and I grew up with two older sisters," Jack said.

Walter had one hand pressed against his nose to stop the bleeding. He held the other out to Jack. "I owe you." He turned to leave.

Rachel hung back. She grabbed Jack and kissed him hard. "Call me," she whispered.

CHAPTER THREE

When Jack discovered diving and spearfishing as a young boy, it was a new world for him. He'd spent most of his life reading and daydreaming about treasure. His spare moments were spent in the Panama Canal Library, reading old books and accounts of pirates looting Spanish ships, especially off Panama's coast. Treasure awaited in the Pearl Islands of Panama, and he knew one day he would find it.

He had found a gold coin once, and every time he looked at it, his heart raced as he thought of finding more. As an adult, he ached to drop everything, even his job, to look for treasure, but he knew he had to plan ahead and save for his dreams of the future.

Unlike most treasure hunters, he didn't care whether or not he became rich. He wanted the thrill of hunting for and finding treasure. Coupling that with his addiction to free diving, he realized he needed a boat for both. After their last trip to Isla Elefante, Jack had sold the *Toulouse* to help finance his venture.

He had built a work shed on the Diablo flats on the bank of the Panama Canal. He crammed it with every machine and tool he could scrape up and began to build the boat he'd always wanted. Jack constructed a functional room in the shed with a shower, toilet, and sink for Juan and paid him as watchman. With his son gone, Juan needed the company as much as he needed the work.

Juan was twice Jack's age but always called him Mistah Jack. Juan was dependable, punctual, and honest. They worked on the boat whenever they had the chance. For Jack that would have meant every waking hour he wasn't at his job. He didn't have much of a social life.

Jack had known some women in a few affairs but nothing had ever lasted for more than a day or two. In the past, Jack never had time for romance. He was a loner, and he told himself he liked it that way. The girls took notice, however, as his blond hair darkened and his skinny arms became muscular. He lost his virginity to the leopard lady at the Villa Amor, the best whorehouse in Panama City. She knew it was his first time, so she let him go twice. He loved it, but he never went back when he discovered diving and spearfishing.

It was two months after he saw Rachel when Jack finally finished his boat. He threw a small christening party. Paul, the Dude, Juan, and many of the friends he had gotten to know in Diablo showed up.

With a beer in his hand, Jack asked Juan to speak to everyone. "Okay, Juan, what are you going to name the boat?"

"Mahn, you put me in bad position in front of hall dese peoples. I doan know what to name a boat." Juan was full of fire water and feeling bold. "In Pinogana, where I born, dey have dis fish dat puff up. You eat dis fish an' you dead to rass from poison, an' when e puff up even de shaak kyant bite 'im. So, I names she de *Arugaduga*!"

Everyone cheered and clapped as Juan spelled out the name on the light gray hull in black magic marker. It would later be painted over in black, just as Juan had written it. One of the Dude's girlfriends slammed a bottle of beer on it, and it was officially launched.

The boat was as good as Juan and Jack could make it. She was twenty-two-feet long and powered by two one-hundred-horsepower Mercury outboard motors. She was fast, but nothing that would win a race. Her fiberglass hull had enough Kevlar and titanium sheets to make it almost bulletproof. It had stowable fish boxes, lockers, and even a pull-out sleeping cover for the rain. Her twin, below-deck fuel tanks carried sixty gallons each, with jugs that could be tied to the railing for more. She had a center console rigged for fishing or diving, with a retractable dive platform. The perfect dive boat, it was low to the water, but it was wide, with a cutting deep "V" hull for sharp turns and a sloping cigarette boat bow. She danced over three-foot chop at thirty knots. In calm seas, the *Arugaduga* was capable of about thirty-five knots. After a few sea trials, Jack knew he had the boat he had always wanted. The *Arugaduga* would win no beauty contests, but she was seaworthy.

Jack, Paul, the Dude and an old high school friend, Pete Hernandez, went for a few diving trips to try her out. Pete wasn't a swimmer, so they had trained him to handle the boat. He became such an excellent driver, they made him permanent captain. Pete actually loved the water as long as he was above it. While he thought all divers were crazy, he admired them and never passed up a chance to go out with his three friends.

One Saturday evening just after dark, Jack was at the shed making some small improvements on the *Arugaduga*. Juan had gone home to Nuevo Vijilla for the weekend. Everyone else who owned a shed had packed it in. A car pulled up and Jack heard someone walking toward the open doors. He stopped midway down the the boat's stepladder when he saw Rachel Mendoza walk through the door.

She looked around. "Some setup," she said.

"Rachel, what are you doing here?"

"You never called me. I just wanted to see what you were up to."

"Where's Walter?"

"Where do you think? He's out on his toy boat, fishing, drinking with his friends, and I'm sure, having sex with one of the many girls they always bring with them."

"Aw, c'mon, Rachel, Walter's not like that."

"You're not married to him."

"He just doesn't seem like that kind of guy. I mean, with a beautiful woman like you, who could need more?"

"That's just it. Walter can never get enough of anything. He always has to have the most of the best."

"He certainly has that in you."

Jack stepped down from the ladder but kept his distance. He wasn't sure how to read Rachel, and he didn't trust himself if he got too close to her.

"You're sweet, but I'll tell you something because I know you don't talk around. Walter and I haven't slept together in the same bed as man and wife for almost five years now. I don't let him put his hands on me, and he doesn't even try anymore. He likes his *putas* better, anyway."

"God, that's unbelievable." Jack wiped his hands with a rag. "You still go places with him, though."

"One has to keep up appearances."

Jack definitely noticed her appearance. She dressed seductively with her form-fitting short skirt and loose blouse exposing just enough of her voluptuous breasts to catch Jack's attention. The more Jack looked at her, the more spellbound he became. "So . . . so, what're you up to tonight?"

"I thought I'd come over here and take you for a ride. We could talk and keep each other company. Unless you're busy?"

"No . . . no . . . I mean, no."

Rachel laughed and shook her head. Her red hair fell across her face. "Don't worry, Jack, I won't bite you."

"I wouldn't care if you did." Jack regained his composure.

"How long until you're finished?"

"I was finished as soon as you walked through that door."

"Well, clean up and let's get out of here."

Jack quickly showered, dressed, and secured the doors. He couldn't believe she wanted to be with him. He slid into the front seat of her car.

"So, where to?"

"I thought we'd take a ride out to the causeway and talk."

"Sounds great to me."

Rachel drove to an isolated parking lot off the causeway, turned off the engine and lights, and leaned back in her seat.

"That was a real beating you gave to those two rats at the dock."

"I couldn't let those scumbags beat up on my friends."

"Where did you get that temper? Were you always like that?"

"Ha! I used to get chased home from school almost every day, but as I got older, I learned to defend myself. I learned movements and holds, how to punch, and when to let loose with a swift kick in the nuts. That's a real downer for the other guy."

"You were wonderful."

"They were just a couple of bums that didn't know their asses from their heads."

Rachel moved quickly in the darkness and put her hands on both sides of his face, then pressed her warm lips to his. Her passionate and hungry kisses left Jack stunned and breathless. When he recovered, he responded with a fire he had never felt before.

"No, Jack, wait. Not here." Rachel buttoned up her blouse. "We're going somewhere else."

They sped through Panama City, then out into the suburbs. Rachel turned off the main highway and drove through a myriad of back streets leading to a potholed, macadam road. She pulled an automatic garage door opener out of her glove compartment and pressed it. A wrought iron gate swung open in front of a moderate, Spanish-style house, then the garage door opened upward and she drove into the garage. Both the gate and the garage door closed behind them.

"This is my getaway house. It's where I come when I want to be alone or I can't stand Walter anymore. It was once my dad's. That's all he had when he died. I've kept it up with the help of Antonia, my live-in caretaker. I had this house before Walter, and he still doesn't know it exists. Antonia disappears when I come in, unless I call for her."

She took him by the hand and led him into the bedroom. A huge, king-sized bed graced the dimly lit room. Everything was spotless, clean. He took her face in his hands and kissed her softly, tenderly, suppressing his raging desire. She kissed back, gently, almost with restraint. Then the lust that begins in a secret place surfaced. It raced up both their bodies and exploded between them. They tore at each other's clothes, undressing each other. Jack lifted Rachel onto the bed, kissing her entire body. She responded eagerly. He had never felt such excruciating pleasure with another woman before and lost himself in her.

Finally, thoroughly spent, they lay entwined in each other's arms for a long while, breathing heavily. They parted slowly, rolling over onto their backs. There was a long moment of silence between them.

"That was beyond amazing." Rachel struggled to talk while gasping for breath.

"I'm sure you say that to all the guys."

"There are no other guys. You're absolutely wonderful."

"You're so beautiful, I can't believe I just made love to you."

"Well, you sure did." Rachel sat up. She leaned toward Jack, softly pressing her inviting breasts on his chest. Then she sat upright and straddled him, slowly moving her hips.

"You're looking for trouble, woman," Jack said with a devilish grin on his face.

"I'll take all of that kind of trouble I can get." Rachel laughed.

"But what about Walter?"

"What about him?" Rachel slid down beside Jack and laid her head on his chest.

"Well, he's still your husband."

"On paper only." She became quiet. Finally she asked, "Do you know how it all happened?"

"Tell me," he said, taking her hand and drawing her closer to him.

"My maiden name is McLaren. I was born in a small town in the north of Scotland called Inverness.

"After my mother died, my father left Scotland with me when I was about two. We went to Jamaica, then Panama. My dad was a real drinker. Anyway, he met some rich Panamanian businessmen in the course of his carousing. He'd take me to their parties occasionally. When I turned eighteen, all of these rich bastards wanted me to marry their sons. Good ol' Dad, seeing a way to get out of debt and to live an easier life with all the booze he could hold, offered me up to the highest bidder. I didn't want to get married. I wasn't ready to be a wife. Besides, I wanted to pick my own man. Well, the Mendozas had a lot of money and a son who was twenty-one. Walter was nice and charming back then. We went out together a few times, and he was the perfect gentleman—fun to be with, too. Eventually, I consented to marry him. My father was ecstatic. I even thought it was a good idea.

"Things went along fine for a few years, until he began coming home late, drunk, and with perfume and lipstick on his shirts. I was enraged at first, but it happened so many times that I just didn't care anymore. I figured if Walter wanted his putas, he wasn't about to get me, and that was the end of it. I never let him into my bed again. We're more or less cordial to each other, and I go out with him on the boat occasionally, but no more conjugal visits. And worse yet, do you know what his specialty is now?"

Jack shook his head.

"Coke. The damn fool is into cocaine. He's not only going to lose his mind, but he's going to lose his life. He's mixed up with some of those bastards that make and distribute the shit. Sometimes I'm afraid to go out in the boat with him. I swear, he's going to fuck up someday and they're going to kill him."

Rachel wrapped the sheet around her and got out of bed. "Well, that's my sob story. No more history lesson."

"I figured those guys on the float who smacked him around were drug dealers."

"They were just the flunkies. The real bastard is Diego Pinzon, the one they call El Gigante. If he makes a drug deal and the other party doesn't hold up his end of the bargain, they usually end up floating in the Bay of Panama with a necktie—a slit throat with the tongue pulled through it. Nice guys. That's the kind of lovely company Walter is hanging out with. I just don't want to be there when they give him a necktie party. They're all Colombians, too, and they definitely don't fuck around."

"I know all about Pinzon. He had my friend's son killed. Promise me you'll stay away from those guys. I don't want to see you get hurt. I'll help you any way I can."

"Jack Savage, do you have any more sex left in you?" Rachel unwrapped the sheet she had tied around herself.

"More than I can control."

"Let's see if we can get rid of enough so you can get your control back."

This time their lovemaking was smooth and gentle. The fierce urgency was gone but something deeper took its place. They already knew each other's bodies, each other's rhythms. Jack felt as if he were close to having an out-of-body experience of pure pleasure.

Afterward, when they were back in the car, Jack asked, "So how well do you know El Gigante?"

"I only met him once as he was walking down the Balboa Yacht Club pier with his scabby friends. He made some comment to me, but I looked the other way and walked on. He's a mean sonofabitch."

"You've got to steer clear of any of them. If you have trouble, come to me."

"Who else, but to my handsome, brave protector?" She put her head back to be kissed.

He kissed her good night and brushed her cheek with his hand. She smiled at him and drove away.

Jack didn't sleep well that night. The thought of his sex with Rachel repeated itself again and again in his mind. He wanted her with him now, in his bed. He couldn't understand the hold she had on him. He didn't think he could fall in love with this woman. For all he knew, she could be the biggest liar in the world. There was something about her that worried him, but he just couldn't figure out what it was.

The long dive trip coming up was just what he needed.

CHAPTER FOUR

Pete steered the *Arugaduga* for the shortcut to Elefante Island through the pass to the right of Mogo Mogo Island and to the left of Boyaneros. The islands sparkled like emeralds in the blue setting of the ocean with white beaches for bezels. It was worth a rough trip to see them. Jack, Paul, and the Dude arranged their diving gear and drank beer.

Another boat, the *Zackarack*, was running down to the islands with them. It was Zack Martin's boat, and he had three friends on board. Jack was suspicious of Zack and his crew, especially when they asked to accompany them on this trip.

For one thing, Zack didn't like the Dude. The Dude exuded sex appeal. His lust was insatiable, and his classic good looks—blond hair and blue eyes—were irresistible. His motto was, "The difference between friends and acquaintances is their wives."

One of those acquaintances was Zack. He had a gorgeous wife, Millie. She had lustrous, black hair that fell past her shoulders and danced about her as she talked or moved. Her straight nose and sultry, black eyes complimented her full mouth meant for kissing. Although she had a large frame, her figure had the curves and lines of a model. Zack was always too busy drinking and running around in his boat to do his homework. The Dude did it for him. The Dude had met Millie at a typical Zonie party. Zack was drunk, and Millie was disgusted and sitting alone, brooding, when the Dude appeared in front of her. Soon after, they became lovers.

Jack wasn't sure if Zack knew. Gossip traveled fast in the Canal Zone, but maybe Zack didn't like the Dude because sober or drunk, Zack didn't like anyone.

Both boats went down to the islands on water smooth as silk with the sun coming up over Chitre Island fast and hot. It was rainy season and the water was warm. Pete drove while everyone chugged beer.

The Dude was up on the bow looking for something. "Over there, a shark! Head on over there, Pete, then cut the engine and glide up to it. I'm gonna cannonball 'im."

Pete slid up behind the shark, a hammerhead about eight feet long. At the right moment, the Dude was in the air in the cannonball position and landed in back of the shark's dorsal fin with a huge explosion. The startled shark darted into the deep. The Dude pulled himself back onto the boat.

Suddenly a shot popped from the *Zackarack*. Shotgun pellets missed the Dude but hit the side of the boat and caught Paul in his arms, chest, and side of the face. It was bird shot but still stung. Paul was pissed.

Jack said into the radio, "You fuckers are drinking rum, and it's too early for that shit." Jack turned to Paul. "Get me that Mossberg shotgun under the console." He looked at Pete. "Head for them."

Jack had #2 birdshot in his pump gun. When they got close enough, Jack took out their windshield. The *Zackarack* occupants hit the deck.

Then the *Arugaduga* turned in a tight circle, and Jack wiped out their kicker motor with two blasts. Pete got back on course, and Jack yelled into the radio, "Still wanna fuck around?"

"Hey, man, you crazy?"

"Yeah, very crazy. Wanna see more?"

"Hey, cool it, Jack. You shot the hell out of my boat."

"And you shot the hell out of Paul Delsey. That ain't funny."

"Geez, I didn't know we hit anyone. We were playing around."

"Are we still gonna play cowboys and Indians, or are we gonna call a truce?"

"Hey, tell Paul we're sorry, huh?"

"Yeah."

"Maann, you really shot the shit outta my boat." Zack repeated himself over the radio.

"Fuck you!"

Jack, Paul and the Dude dove at Elefante with no luck. They needed to find another spot. Jack looked over toward Monte Island.

"There it is," he said. "I swear I see the clear blue line ahead. Start the engines." As a boy, Jack had once spotted a mile-long line of sardines swimming nose to tail just beneath the ocean surface. The glimmer of their scales drew a clear blue line across the sea, a sign that bigger fish and good times were not far behind. He had been searching for it ever since.

"Damn, Jack, you're always seeing that fuckin' clear blue line, an' when we get there, there ain't shit." The Dude laughed.

"You'll see. You'll see. There's fish there. I just know it."

Pete steered straight for Jack's line and stopped the boat.

"Yeah, mud," Paul mumbled.

The clear blue line, the one perfect spot Jack had spent his life chasing, was a phantom again. The water was cloudy, but at least there were fish.

The Dude was the first one in and immediately shot a big amberjack. It gave him a hard time for a while, but just as he popped his head up the third time for a quick gasp of air and a wave of his gun to the boat, a large tiger shark came out of the murk and grabbed his fish. The shark swallowed it whole. The Dude struggled to pull his spear shaft and detachable point out of the fish in the shark's mouth, but it wouldn't budge and he was towed behind. He was headed for the other boat.

The Dude grabbed the side of the *Zackarack* and tried to hand someone his gun, so he could climb aboard. Instead of helping him, they laughed and kicked at him, stomping his hands.

The tiger shark swallowed the fish and turned back toward the Dude. He jammed the end of his speargun into the shark's mouth, deflecting its rush, but the shark sandpapered the Dude's side with its toothy, rasp-like skin. The Dude spun completely around.

Paul had seen enough. He slipped into the water with the three rubbers cocked on his speargun and the detachable point off of the end of the shaft. He didn't want to be connected to any monster like that after he shot it.

No one swam like Paul. He was at the Dude's side almost immediately. The big shark made another turn. The Dude's gun was now a crunched, aluminum tube. Paul lay ready in the water for the next attack. The shark went for the Dude. Paul had positioned himself far enough away from the direct line of attack but close enough to get a good shot. The big tiger shark charged not four feet from him, and the silver shaft ripped into its gills as it passed. The shark went out of control. It smacked Paul with its tail as it twisted and turned, then it slammed into the boat like a runaway torpedo, sending some of the occupants to the deck. Paul pulled his shaft out. He and the Dude swam back to the *Arugaduga*. They stopped to watch as the tiger shark spun and looped in circles, deeper and deeper to its eventual death in the abyss.

"*Zackarack*," Jack said over the radio, "that was a very naughty thing to do. There's someone here who has something to say to you."

Paul spoke with his usual calm. "You are challenged to a shark jumping contest, so do your leg stretches and say your prayers. We're anchoring at Ensenada tonight, home of the tiger shark. We'll save all our fish carcasses for chum. Meet us there. Start hitting the rum heavily for bravery. Out."

This conversation could be heard by anyone in Panama who had a radio. The people at the Balboa Yacht Club bar listened with great enjoyment.

"You guys're asses," Zack called back. "We'll be there!" Beneath the bravado, they could all hear his fear.

"Both of you look like you've taken twenty lashes with steel wool," Jack said.

"Man, that shark had tough skin." The Dude held up his arm to look at his side.

"I thought that sonofabitch was gonna hit me for a home run with its tail," Paul said, inspecting his own wounds.

"Hey, Paul, thanks," the Dude said.

Paul dismissed the incident and reached into the cooler for a beer.

"Grab me one too, huh?" the Dude said.

"I yank your ass away from being shark bait and now I have to wait on you, too?"

"Ah, shit, I'll get it."

"Can't you take a joke?" They all laughed as Paul threw a beer to the Dude.

After a long day of diving, Pete drove the *Arugaduga* to the anchorage off the little palm-studded, thatched-roof town of Ensenada on the southern end of Rey Island. It was the best place in the islands for tiger sharks.

They cleaned the fish they shot that day and stored the filets in the built-in coolers. Afterward, they readied heavy shark lines for the evening's game.

"The reason why the tiger shark is the most dangerous shark in the ocean is its size and eating habits. They grow larger than the white shark, have the largest mouth of all the predator sharks, and will eat anything, living or dead, just about any time. Their teeth are serrated and at right angles, so that anything they bite down on gets punctured, sliced, or crunched."

"Now ain't Paul the professor," the Dude said.

"Afraid of learning something?" Jack said.

Paul ignored them. He loved fishing and diving and he had spent most of his life learning everything thing he could.

He continued. "One captive tiger shark's stomach contents revealed three rolls of tar paper, other sharks, sting rays, plastic bags of garbage, two pelicans, human remains, and a monkey. They'll attack and eat anything. One of their favorites is chomping on giant sea turtles, which can sometimes be as big as four feet across. A tiger shark can crunch chunks out of body and shell, then return for more until it's all gone. I've heard of them being twenty to twenty-five feet long."

"Makes it sound like there's nothing to worry about," the Dude said.

"I'd be more afraid of Zack if I were you," Paul said. "Messing around with another man's wife is worse than asking for trouble." He looked to Jack for agreement. Jack didn't look back.

After they finished filleting, Jack tied three large fish carcasses onto the shark lines, threw them into the water, and cleated them off below the surface.

"Hey, *Zackarack*. You guys still coming over to our little party here at Ensenada?" Jack said over the radio. There was a moment of silence.

An unenthusiastic answer finally came back. "Yeah, yeah, we're here. We're on our way in."

About an hour later, the *Zackarack* appeared at the mouth of the bay and pulled up to the *Arugaduga*.

The Dude was still furious but kept it to himself. Paul was stoically silent while Jack had a big smile on his face.

THE CLEAR BLUE LINE   37

"Fancy meeting you here in this lonely bay of bats, pirates, and tiger sharks," Jack said. "C'mon and tie up to us and share some booze and chow and shoot the breeze."

The *Zackarack* anchored and both boats tied up side by side. Two paddles were tied down, one at the bow and one at the stern, so that their lengths held the boats apart. Even though there was no love lost between the two crews, they were cordial and talked across to each other as if nothing had happened.

"Catch anything today?" Jack asked.

"A lot of bonita at first but later a few dolphin. Bob and Frank each caught nice wahoos," Zack answered. "What did you guys get?"

"Some good-sized amberjack, but Paul, never to be outdone, nailed about a seventy-pound dogtooth. We're loaded."

"Yeah, I shot myself a nice-sized tiger shark, too," Paul said.

"Ha! Yeah, and I was the bait for it. Whaddaya think a that?" The Dude laughed.

One of the shark lines tugged at the cleat, then the other. The boats rocked and moved around. The tiger sharks had arrived. There were no hooks on the lines, just tied carcasses of the big fish they had shot. When one was bitten off, another was tied on. It was dark by now, and the men needed flashlights to see down into the deep chasm between the boats. Two big tiger sharks tore at the bait. They thrashed the water and shook their blunt heads back and forth, crunching through the big fish carcasses, bone, and heavy tuna line.

"Oops! Gonna need another coupl'a big carcasses for these hungry little darlings. They just finished their appetizers," the Dude said.

He and Pete pulled the sliced-off lines into the boat and each tied a carcass on by the tail. They hung them over the side so the tips of the heads were in the water. Everyone shone their lights on the fish carcasses. A tiger shark's cruel head exploded through the dark water. It tore off half a carcass and slammed into the boat. They all jumped backward. The Dude, whose line was the target of the shark, was bending over jiggling the bait when the big shark attacked it. It missed his head by a foot. He leaped up, fell backward, and sat down in surprise.

"I thought the bastard was coming into the boat after me."

The crew of the *Zackarack* was impressed. They passed around another bottle of rum. More bait was put out the same way, and more sharks performed. They got the carcasses every time.

"You guys ready for a visitor?" Paul called out to the other boat. Before anyone could answer, he leaped over the canyon of death and landed on the *Zackarack*. He took a chug of beer, looked at the four fishermen, then turned and jumped over the feeding sharks onto the *Arugaduga*. The Dude was next. He stood on the side of the boat with a fish in his hand.

"Rover, rover, let the Dude come over." He put the large fish in his mouth, biting through its skin and flew over to the other boat. He teetered a bit, turned, and leaped back. Then he turned the fish around, bit down on its tail, leaned over the side, and hung there, the fish barely touching the surface.

"Dude! You damn fool!" Jack yelled. "Don't do it!" It was too late. A shark rushed out of the dark, lunged through the surface of the water, and tore the fish out of The Great Spearin' Dude's mouth. He fell back onto the deck again.

"That had to be one of the dumbest tricks I've ever seen." Paul scratched his head. "What you been smokin'?"

"He's fuckin' drunk. I've got to get going before I lose my audience." Jack stood on the side of the boat, made a rooster call, and jumped across to the other boat. He landed evenly on the side but slipped on some fish slime. He slid along the side on his back. Jack grabbed the boat with his right hand and stopped himself as he was about to land on top of the sharks.

All hands on the *Zackarack* were laughing.

"Neat trick." Jack smiled. "Greasing the landing zone with fish slime makes for a funny landing, doesn't it?"

It was dark, but they didn't have to see Jack to know how angry he was. He calmly picked up a wet rag lying on the deck and wiped off his feet, then wiped off the place where he landed and slipped. He squeezed the rag into a hard ball, smiled at Zack, and threw it into his face hard. Zack traveled backward and dropped his drink. He wiped his face but said nothing. Jack leaped to the top of the boat in one movement, then jumped back to his boat.

"Those bastards on the *Zackarack* are whacked out on weed or coke. They must have picked up some of that Panama Red that grows right here on Rey Island," Paul said.

"C'mon. Return the favor. Jump your wimpy asses over here for a visit," Jack called to them.

The *Zackarack* was silent. Paul and the Dude joined in the taunting. Pete kept out of it. Another shark slammed into the boat.

"Well, guess y'guys ain't comin' over," the Dude called out into the dark. He was calling out on the wrong side of the boat.

"Hey, dumbass, over here," Jack said.

The Dude turned around and staggered to the other side of the boat.

"Wait!" A cry came out of the dark from the *Zackarack*. It was Zack. "I'll do it!" He was doped and soused to the gills. With great effort, he climbed up onto the top side of his boat. He stood there like the great white whale, no shirt, his large, round belly hanging down. He glowed in the dark. He held onto the corner of the *Zackarack*'s canvas top and swayed unsteadily.

The crew of the *Arugaduga* looked at Zack, then at each other. Almost in one voice they yelled, "Don't do it!"

"Gotta stop that asshole from jumping. He'll be shark bait if he does." Jack saw how wasted Zack was. Even sober he was in such bad physical condition that he could never make the jump. "Don't jump, Za—"

It was too late. Zack was in the air before Jack could finish his warning. The crew of the *Arugaduga* watched as if hypnotized at the approach of an ungainly, white mass. Suddenly, it stopped approaching and began to descend. His belly bounced like a basketball off the side of the boat, and the blubbery mess entered the water in a giant explosion.

"I'll get 'immm!" the Dude yelled and jumped into the water. Zack screamed hysterically. The Dude grabbed Zack by the hair, and with the help of his adrenaline, swam the large cargo to the dive platform. Waiting hands jerked Zack out of the water just in time for the Dude to sit up on the platform and kick a big shark in the nose. He tucked his legs up as another shark bounced off the back of the platform.

Zack was so terrified he wouldn't go back to his own boat that night, even though they offered to pull up to the side so he could walk over. He wouldn't even move from where he lay on the deck. They managed to get a spare air mattress under him and cover him with a blanket and a poncho. He was shivering from cold and fear.

"What do you think of Zack's first solo flight?" Paul said.

"It didn't go well. I don't think he'll get his flying license this trip."

It rained hard, but the Dude and Zack slept in it.

The next morning was breathtaking. Jack looked over to the mainland, fifty miles away, and watched the morning clouds feel their way around the blue mountains. He knew that one of the mountains was where Balboa first saw the Pacific Ocean. In later years, after Balboa, the Spanish loaded their galleons with treasure plundered from the Aztecs in Peru and sailed up the slot between the Pearl Islands and the mainland to Panama City. Many pirates had hidden out in the Pearl Islands to prey upon the Spanish treasure ships. They attacked the Spanish again and again. As long as there was treasure, there would be pirates. When the Spanish caught a pirate, he was tortured, then executed. There was no mercy on either side. One day, Jack knew he'd have to go after treasure himself, not as a pirate, but as a hunter of the lost gold that had caused so much bloodshed.

Paul was already up, beer in hand.

"How about tossing me a beer?" Jack said. Paul reached into the cooler and threw one to Jack. "Ah, tastes like shit but feels so good."

"It'll build you a new personality."

"Just set back the hangover another day. We've got a long trip home. Might want to get some lobsters on the way back. You know all the places. We'll just tie some tuna cord around your ankle and send you down a hundred feet for some of the big ones. You get two armfuls, tug on the line, and we'll pull you up. Meanwhile," Jack continued, "let's wake up the Dude and get this whale sleeping next to him off the boat."

"Sounds good to me." Paul kicked the Dude while Jack woke up Zack.

Zack didn't know where he was or even who he was. He couldn't focus his eyes, and when he stuck his tongue out, he couldn't get it back into his mouth. It looked like a Gila monster's tail. At least he had the decency to barf over the side. Pete started the engines while Paul pulled up the anchor. As they bumped into the other boat, they announced their captain was coming aboard, bent him over the side of his boat, and shoved.

They left the disoriented crew of the *Zackarack* and headed toward home. Diving for lobsters on the way took longer than expected, and when they passed Pachequilla and headed out into the wide open, it was late afternoon. The hazy and oppressive weather heated the wind around the moving boat. The surface of the water reflected the clouds in a perfect mirror image. They couldn't see a horizon. Pete steered and eyeballed the compass at the same time.

"Hey, Dude. That stunt last night was crazy," Pete said. "Aren't you ever afraid of dying?"

"Don't know, never tried it." The Dude wasn't much for introspection, especially with a hangover.

"Ah, quit fuckin' around, man. I'm serious."

"Well, I did get scared once."

"Yeah, like how?"

"I went to a buddy's funeral. He committed suicide. I was the only

one there. When I went up to the coffin, I saw that it was cockeyed on
its perch. I went to straighten the thing up and the whole damn box 'n
stand'n shit fell over an' broke apart. His body rolled out right in fronta
me. Chucha madre! Whatta sight. Th' sonofabitch wasn't even cleaned
up, an' he had a hundred bullet holes in 'im. He had one eye open an' was
starin' right at me. I turned around an' hauled ass. To this day I still can't
figure out how he managed to shoot himself so many times."

"Oh man, what a story."

"No, no. It's the God's honest truth. I think the bastard was murdered."

"What I meant was, how can you jump around over sharks and shit like
that, jumping in the water with them? Doesn't it scare you?"

"Nah. That's what the booze's for," the Dude said. "You can do
anything with booze."

"Thank God I don't drink." Pete shook his head.

The Dude looked over at Jack. "Whatta time, huh?"

Jack looked at Paul and smiled. "Well, Paul, did you have a good time?"

"Not very exciting, but enjoyable."

"When I think of the sight of Zack flying across to us, I start laughing
again."

"Yeah, when he hit the side of the boat, it sounded like an exploding
water balloon. What'd you think, Dude?" Paul said.

"It was really hairy. I couldn't believe I was in the water with 'im an'
the sharks. Man, I ain't gonna fuck his wife no more . . . an' I ain't gonna
fuck her no less, either." Everyone laughed.

Jack thought about Rachel. He still couldn't believe he slept with her.
He found himself craving her again.

"Hey, Jack . . . Jack. What're ya doin', dreamin'?" The Dude poked him.
Jack shook his head and looked up.

"Oh, shit," Jack said.

"Oh, shit, what?" Dude asked.

"Look ahead of us."

"Ain't nothin' there."

"See those cumulus clouds? We left too late."

CHAPTER FIVE

A calm return to the mainland was always a pleasant gift—a little sun, some fluffy clouds, and a flat, calm sea. With the throttle down almost all the way, the boat would lift on a plane and skim across a passive ocean. But the beauty can become a beast. Though harmless looking from a distance, the picturesque cumulous clouds would build up into thunderheads that rimmed the coast of the mainland for a hundred miles. Jack had been fooled before by these scenic balls of cotton. They could rise thousands of feet from the damp earth of the tropics, sucking huge amounts of moisture with them, until they flattened at around forty thousand feet in the shape of an anvil. Unable to hold more water, the giant clouds would purge themselves, releasing rain in wild, windblown torrents. They generated their own energy, drawing in air from all around them. The ocean followed suit as the wind rushing to and from the maelstrom tore the surface apart.

They were in for wild rain, pure wind, and crazy lightning.

"Look at that line squall heading our way," Paul said.

"Yep, and it's a beaut. It's already spitting lightning and we're the highest object around," Jack said.

"So?"

"So, we're going to haul ass until we run out of smooth water. When the shit hits, we're going to hunker down, idle ahead slow, wait for the wind and the rain, and pray to God that the lightning doesn't hit us."

When the white line from the storm approached, it was wind, rain, and whitecaps on an angry sea gone wild. As it hit, the boat shuddered and the wind blew the rain so hard it stung the skin like jabbing needles. Vision was limited. The piercing rain drops turned into sharp missiles, blinding whoever looked ahead.

Pete pushed the throttle down all the way, eating up as much of the calm water as he could before the storm. The surface of the water began to take on a brushed texture as the wind increased. Small waves formed. They increased in size as the storm drew closer. There was no choice out in the big middle. The line squall stretched too far to run around, and running back was out of the question. A solid wall of whitecaps headed their way.

"I've never seen anything like it," Jack said. "When that wind hits, it's going to be a bitch."

The first blast of wind almost tore the ragtop off the boat. Pete cut down on the speed. The next couple of gusts were even more violent. Pete struggled with the wheel to keep the boat on course. He cut it down to a slow idle. The ragtop ripped off with a loud report and slapped into the water, held only by some, always dependable, tuna cord. Jack went to retrieve it but it began to whiplash around dangerously. It was a chore to maneuver around the boat in the grip of the worsening seas. The remainder of the cloth top churned in the water and swirled around in the turbulence of the outboard engines. Jack grabbed a knife. He knew if the canvas top fouled the props, the engines would seize up and they'd be in more trouble. He cut the line and watched as the canvas spun in the wash for a while, then drifted off.

"Hey, Pete, cut off an engine and we'll just run on one until we're through this."

Pete cut off an engine as the full force of the storm hit. A giant wave crashed over the bow like a waterfall; everything not secured was tangled, smashed together, and washed overboard. The divers held on grimly.

The Dude and Paul were tossed into the ocean and disappeared fast. "Pete! Turn around, we've lost two!"

Pete swung around hard to port. The boat wallowed and began to broach as it turned sideways in the trough of the wave. The *Arugaduga* was in a rollover position and taking water over the down side. She would capsize in a moment, but Pete, hanging onto the wheel, maneuvered the boat along the wall of the wave, and turning at the right time, surfed their way to safety. With a following sea, he plowed his way toward the two bobbing heads. It was difficult maneuvering the *Arugaduga* into position to pick them up, but Pete had become a master at handling the boat. After a few passes and wave collisions, the Dude and Paul were on board. The storm was still ahead of them. Another wave engulfed them as they all grabbed for a hold. When the wave cleared, Jack was holding onto Paul's T-shirt, and Paul was hanging off the outboard engine. His shirt looked like it was about seven feet long. Jack yanked him back aboard as another wave hit. They dove to the deck and grabbed at anything.

"Pete, fire up the other engine!" Jack yelled.

"I already did!"

Pete held the *Arugaduga* dead ahead, idling up and over the crests of the vicious waves. They took a beating for about another hour, then the rain lashed down at them. The rain was so strong it tore the whitecaps off the big waves, and the seas began to settle down. Visibility was zero.

"Damn, these fuckin' raindrops sting like buckshot," the Dude said.

A deafening blast of thunder suddenly exploded from somewhere in the rain. Everyone jumped.

"What was that?"

"We're in the lightning!" Paul yelled. "Try not to hold onto anything metal." The words were hardly spoken when everything seemed to light up. Brilliant light danced around the boat for a few seconds and was gone. Everyone was down. Pete was slumped over the wheel. The boat was still moving ahead slowly. The other three were lying in different positions on the deck. Jack got to his feet first. He held his chest and winced. The other two began to move and eventually got up. Jack looked over at the steering wheel.

"Pete!" He rushed over to his unconscious friend and grabbed him by the shoulders, shaking him hard. Pete moaned.

Paul grabbed Pete's legs. They laid him on the deck and shook him again. Fortunately, Pete came around.

"Sonofabitch looks like someone hit 'im in th' head with a baseball bat," the Dude said.

"You always say the right thing at the wrong time." Paul shook his head.

In spite of their clumsy efforts, they managed to revive Pete and get him back on his feet. Although every one of them felt like they had been mauled, Pete had been hit the hardest. The force of the lightning had come straight through the wheel. It was a miracle no one had been killed and that the engines kept running.

"You take a break, Pete. I'll take her in," Jack said.

Pete sat down on the deck, and the Dude produced his magical bottle of gin.

"I don't drink, Dude."

"This ain't booze, now, it's medicine. Take a slug." Pete took a couple of slugs.

When the storm abated, Jack took the *Arugaduga* the rest of the way at top speed. He called in to a few friends who had radios in their houses and told them about the lightning and Pete's condition. They said they would have someone at the pier to take Pete up to Gorgas Hospital when the boat arrived.

Despite all that had happened, Jack couldn't stop thinking of Rachel all the way back.

They motored into the landing with a crowd waiting for them. The medics carried Pete on a stretcher and took off for the hospital. Paul and the Dude helped put the boat on the trailer and pulled it up to Jack's shed. They cleaned it out, washed it, flushed the engine, sorted out their gear, divvied up the fish, and went home.

Jack stayed behind to square away some equipment. He climbed up into the boat to inspect any damage. It was still in good shape. He could finally go home and rest. He walked to the big sliding doors at the front of the shed. He closed and locked them, then turned to get into his truck.

There stood Rachel. The shock electrified him like a second bolt of lightning.

CHAPTER SIX

"How did you know I was back?" Jack asked.

"I heard it on the radio at the Yacht club. Wanted to make sure you were all right."

"What are you doing at the Yacht club?"

"My husband has a boat, remember? Hey, what're you going to do, give me the third degree?" She pouted.

"I'm sorry, Rachel. Anyway, I'm really glad to see you . . . really glad."

"I feel the same way." Rachel twirled her keys around her finger and smiled. "Care to go somewhere?"

"I'm filthy and fishy. I've got to take a shower first."

"You can take one at my place."

"I've got to get some clean clothes."

"Leave your car here. We'll go in mine."

"You don't mind the fishy smell?"

"Jack, get your ass in the car."

Jack got his clothes and jumped into Rachel's car. "How are things with Walter?"

"Lousy, as usual," she said with disgust.

"Well, how've you been?" He smiled and looked at her face. He was aroused.

"Oh, busy. Running errands all over Panama."

"Yeah, like what?"

"Hey, what is this? What's with all the questions? All you've been doing is grilling me ever since I met you tonight."

Jack could sense a sort of nervousness about Rachel. She wasn't as relaxed as she was on their first meeting. He decided not to ask her anymore questions, but he was sure something was really bothering her. They drove on for some time in silence. If she wants to do something tonight, fine, Jack thought. If she doesn't, fine. If she never wants to do anything ever, well that's just fine, too. He had his own stubborn way of withdrawing.

"Jack, I'm sorry. I've been a little upset today about some private family matters."

Jack sensed there was more, but he let it ride. "That's all right, I was too nosy. I really didn't mean to be. No more questions."

They drove to her getaway house. It was perfectly clean and in order, just as before.

"You must be hungry."

"Well, a little. Don't get much to eat on those diving trips."

"I'll fix you a sandwich while you take a shower."

After the shower, he walked into the kitchen in his fresh change of clothes, barefoot. He came up behind Rachel and kissed her on the neck, while cupping her breasts in his hands. She moaned with delight, then turned, and put her face up to his. What began as a light kiss soon turned into a wild moment of passion.

She pushed herself away from him. "Let's get some food into you first."

Jack ate his sandwich and drank a beer. "Aah, that was good. I needed that."

"Do you want more?"

"Of what?"

"You know what I mean." She giggled.

"And you know what I want."

"And what could that be?"

He plunked his beer bottle down on the table and stood up. With the speed and agility of a cat, he swooped her up in his arms and headed for the bedroom.

"Jaack." She feigned resistance, kicking her feet and struggling playfully.

"You're going to bed, my pretty, and do I have a surprise for you."

"Bet I know what it is." She laughed all the way to the bed.

Their lovemaking was even sweeter this time. They knew each other better now, and everything was smoother, yet more intense. Jack kissed her lovely breasts while caressing her ass. As he entered her, they both exploded in pleasure at the same time, giving to and taking from each other's bodies every ounce of gratification. Even after being spent, their bodies throbbed, refusing to relinquish each other.

They lay next to each other and shared that after-sex relaxation and glow. "Wow, this is getting addictive," Rachel said.

"I hope so."

"I love you, Jack."

Jack was silent. He couldn't believe what he heard. "What did you say?"

"I said, I love you, you dope. You do something to me. You make me all jittery inside when I see you. After we say good-bye, I can't wait to see you again."

"I feel the same way about you, Rachel, but is it love, or are we just craving each other?"

"Maybe a little of both," she said, tickling his ear with a few strands of her hair.

"I think we are in tune with each other's bodies," he said, swatting away the tuft of hair and laughing.

"That's not all that's in tune, big boy." She laughed, pressing herself against his body.

"Why you little . . ." He pinned her beneath him. "You'll pay for that."

"Make me pay."

The Dude already had a hard-on, just thinking about Millie as he drove to her house and parked on Tavernilla Street near Sosa Hill. He couldn't wait to see her.

"Where were you? I was getting ready to leave," Millie said.

"Ah, I had a little trouble gettin' the car started, and then traffic, and—"

Millie grabbed the Dude and laid a kiss on him that took his breath away.

"Damn Sam! Man o man, you're in for it, woman. I'm gonna fuck you until we both go blind and turn into puddin'."

"Promise?"

They drove in the Dude's car to Los Espejos, a nearby push button—one of those temporary short-stop motels where no one asks any questions. The Dude drove into the open carport and a sliding door closed behind them. They both got out of the car and walked to a door on the side of the garage. A small sliding panel opened in the middle of it, and a hand came out, palm up. The Dude laid a ten dollar bill in it. The hand withdrew and the panel slid shut. After the sounds of some scurrying around in the room, a buzzer sounded and the entrance opened.

"Well, I'll be damned—a bordello fit for two sex fiends," Millie said.

There were mirrors everywhere—the walls, the ceilings, even a part of the floor—and the most luxurious bed ever made for the art of sexual endeavor.

"I sure hope you're horny. You're in for it, lover boy." Millie's eyes flashed with desire.

He took off all his clothes. "I don't know if you're up to it. This fucker's angry. I been outta sight'a women for more'n a week, and I'm ready for a nuclear reaction."

"Well, Captain Atomic, c'mon over to the bed and I'll begin your meltdown."

He climbed onto the bed and reached for her. She bounded off and stood facing him. Doing a slow, erotic dance, she began undressing. Her dress dropped, then her slip. Slowly, she unsnapped and dropped her bra, holding onto a strap. She twirled it in front of her before letting it fly into the Dude's face. Either Millie wasn't fast enough or she had orchestrated her scenario perfectly. The Dude lifted her up in his arms and threw her on the bed. He licked his way from her toes to her breasts, then with one, passionate kiss, he wrestled her beneath him. Millie resisted just enough to bring out the fire in the Dude, then met it with a passion of her own.

Their lovemaking went on until there was a loud knock on the wall behind them. Another sliding door opened and a hand came out again.

"I paid them for two hours. What the hell's going on?"

"How long do you think we've been pounding the sheets, Tarzan?"

"We been at it for two hours?"

"Look at your watch."

"Chucha madre. Time flies when you're bein' punished."

"Pay the man, and get ready for some more punishment."

Two hours later, Millie snuggled up to the Dude in his car. "Nick, it's more than just sex between us, right?"

"What kinda question is that?"

"I'm serious. We ought to be married."

"You're talking crazy, now. You know you're already married."

"I'd divorce my drunken husband in a second for you."

"C'mon, let's just enjoy each other."

"I care a lot for you, Nick."

The Dude felt lightheaded, then panicky. He felt like he had a ping pong ball bouncing around in his chest. He began to sweat profusely.

"Millie, please, don't talk like this now."

"Don't you love me?"

"Yeah, yeah, sure."

"You don't sound very convincing."

"Whattam I s'posed t' say? Y' got me between a rock and an ass-breaking hard place."

"Oh, the hell with it. Just get me to my car."

Before she left, the Dude grasped her arm. "Don't be mad. Please."

She yanked her arm away from him and stepped out of the car.

"When can we get together again?" he asked.

Millie turned around. "The next time you have sex with me will be in your mind, with your hand doing the job for you, you asshole." She slammed the door hard, got into her car, and peeled out.

The Great Spearin' Dude sat in his car for some time until another car came up behind him and he had to move on. His inflated male ego was completely out of air.

CHAPTER SEVEN

Paul had, at last, found heaven in lovely, blue-eyed Polly. Five years younger and outgoing, she brought Paul out of his shell. Just like Paul, she was a geologist and a Zonie. And just like Paul, she was in love. The two should have teamed up years ago, but Paul's shyness had kept them apart.

He was brave facing sharks, but around women, Paul was a coward. Women had made passes at him but either he never noticed or was too nervous to respond. He had been in love with Polly Deming, his assistant, for years, but never had the nerve to tell her. He watched Polly's boyfriends come and go and despaired whenever he saw her with someone.

One day, when the two of them were out in the field studying some core samples on top of a hill above the canal, it began to rain a real, tropical, Panama downpour. Paul remembered an old hunter's lean-to in the jungle not far from the clearing they were in. Although only a thatched roof structure in disrepair, it provided shelter from the storm. The leaking roof made it impossible to stay dry, but it was better than being out in the driving rain. Polly shivered. A blast of lightning hit close and loud. She instinctively jumped toward Paul. She wrapped her arms around him tightly, trembling. Paul, slowly, cautiously, put his arms around her and held her to quiet her shaking.

She raised her head and looked up at him. They saw something in each other's eyes neither had seen before. Polly moved her wet face closer to Paul's. Too much of a temptation for even such a timid soul as Paul, he took her face into his hands and kissed her gently. She responded with such passion that all those years of loving each other flooded through them and into their embrace.

Since that day, they couldn't be separated. They went everywhere together. Paul discovered there were other things in life besides his job, reading, and diving. He tried to teach Polly how to dive for lobster and shoot fish, but she got seasick on a boat. On the weekends, she would cook him a lobster and fish meal at his bachelor quarters in Williamson Place in the Canal Zone town of Balboa. Then she would stay the rest of the weekend with him.

After he came home from the last dive trip, shaken and bruised and a little tired of his single buddies, the drinking and the crazy stunts, he knew it was time to settle down. He left the ring under her pillow, afraid if he asked her directly, she might say no.

The Great Spearin' Dude wasn't happy. He felt terrible after his break-up with Millie. He had dated dozens of women in the past, picked them up fast and discarded them just as quickly. But Millie was different—he couldn't get her out of his mind. She was not only the sexiest woman he had ever met, but she also had a fantastic sense of humor. He had never gotten along so well with anyone. He missed her deeply.

He called her when Zack was at work or gone fishing, but she would have nothing to do with him. He wouldn't beg, but it was getting so he couldn't stand it anymore. He couldn't tell her he loved her. That would be against his rules. His rules were his rules, and they couldn't be broken. That's what got him through the orphanage. That's what got him through the Vietnam War. That's what kept him going. That's what made him The Great Spearin' Dude. But just because he couldn't tell her didn't mean it would be bad if someone else did.

"No way," Jack said "Damnit, Dude. Tell her you love her. You've lied before."

"No, that's not it. I think I really do love her."

"Well, then tell her."

"I can't."

"Why not?"

"I just can't, that's all."

"So, I'm supposed to call Millie and tell her 'I love you' for you?"

"Something like that."

"Am I supposed to pimp for you, too?"

"Would you?"

Jack laughed. "You're one funny fucker. Give me her phone number. Hey, Zack had better not answer the phone. I don't like him, and I don't want to give him the pleasure of thinking I'm chasing his wife."

"No sweat. The number's for her duty station at Gorgas. Just ask for her. When you talk to her, give her my number and ask her, or hell, beg her to call me. Please. It's important."

"Chucha madre, Dude, you're throwing me to the sharks. Give me the damn number."

"Hey, Jack, one more thing."

"What now?" Jack rolled his eyes.

"Call me back if she won't call me."

"You gonna tell me you love me?"

"No, man, I just wanna know what she said."

"Give me the number."

When Millie finally did call, she was formal, distant. The Dude had to plead with her to meet him in downtown Panama at a little cafe they both knew. She was late.

"Hey, thanks for meeting me. I really appreciate it big time, Mil." The Dude was nervous.

"So, what's the problem, Nick?"

"I just wanted to see you, that's all, an' shoot the breeze." The Dude didn't know how to explain himself. He didn't know how to admit he could no longer go on without this woman sitting across from him.

"If that's the reason you wanted me to come down here, it's been a big waste of time for both of us." She pushed back from the table and stood up quickly, grabbing her purse.

"No, no, no, I didn't mean it that way," he said, jumping up. "Please, don't leave. I . . . I have something to say."

She stood motionless, looking at him with disdain. Without changing her expression, she slowly dropped back into her chair.

"I just wanted to tell you that I . . . " The Great Spearin' Dude froze. Nothing would come out of his mouth. His lips and tongue moved slightly. He gestured with his hands, but Millie couldn't understand his sign language. Her nursing instincts suggested he might be choking.

"Nick? Nick? Can you breathe?"

He shook his head.

"Are you all right?"

He nodded.

"Is this all you have to say to me?"

He shook his head, then nodded, then shook his head again.

"You sure you're okay?"

He nodded again.

"Then it's good-bye, Great Spearin' Asshole." Millie swiped her purse off the table and got up.

This time he pounded on the table with his fist. He motioned her back to him with his hands. Pointing to his mouth with a finger and making the stop sign, then the prayer sign, he grunted out an inaudible sound.

"What?" Millie sat down and leaned across the table.

Like a stroke victim, he tried desperately to speak.

"I'm going to try once more. What are you trying to tell me?" Millie stared into the Dude's bulging eyes.

"I . . . lo . . . love . . . yo . . . you. I love you, damnit!"

"You love me?"

Once he'd said it, the words flowed freely. "I love you! I love you!"

People in the cafe stared at the couple, but the Dude was on a roll. He ran around the table and brought Millie to her feet, then he kissed her.

Millie looked into the Dude's eyes, and with a joyful smile on her face, laughed. "Oh, Nick."

The whole cafe cheered.

The invitation to the Mendoza's party had arrived two days ago. Jack swore he wasn't going. By the second day, he knew he couldn't resist. When he arrived at Walter's two-story mansion, the butler welcomed him. Soft Latin music flowed from the balcony. He could hear the cacophony of ice cubes clinking in glasses, cocktail shakers, music, laughter, and conversation coming from upstairs.

Walter received Jack with a bear hug and a slap on the back. Jack had a strong twinge of guilt as he returned the greeting. He stepped back and looked at Walter. Walter looked as if he had aged twenty years. He had lost weight drastically. His face was drawn, and his eyes had a terrified expression, like a dog with his balls caught in a rat trap. It seemed to Jack that Walter really didn't want to be at this party either. Walter looked around nervously, not really paying attention to Jack. Jack finally got his attention.

"You all right, Walter?"

"I'm fine," he said. "Just checking out the party to see if everyone is okay."

"Anything I can help you with?"

Walter laughed. "If there's trouble, I know you can help. I'll never forget that day on the dock." Suddenly he grabbed Jack's forearm in a tight grip. He spoke quietly, to mask his voice. "I can depend on you, can't I?"

"You just say the word."

"Okay, okay. Now you go have a good time. Have fun." With that, Walter turned to someone else and continued his charade of cheerfulness.

Jack milled around, talking to people and drinking beer. He was anxious to see Rachel, but she was lost somewhere in the crowd. He talked to a few Panamanian women and marveled at how beautiful the women of Panama were. A few beers later, he ran into Rachel. She was laughing with a group of guests and had turned around to move on, when their eyes met.

"Jack Savage, how nice of you to come," she said. Her act was good.

"It's nice to be here." He feigned innocence.

"I do hope that you have a good time."

"Why, thank you," he answered politely.

"Ciao," she said with a wave and a smile, and disappeared into the crowd.

What the hell was that? Jack thought. She was polite but cool. Jack milled around some more and drank a lot of beer. He wanted to talk to her for a moment, maybe for a hint of their next meeting. He finally saw her off in a corner by herself and went over to her.

"Rachel, what's going on?"

"Nothing's going on. I have guests to greet." She brushed past him and walked to the front of the large patio where there was some excitement.

Jack walked slowly, almost paralyzed with hurt, to where the action was. There, in the middle of the crowd of partygoers stood El Gigante.

The Colombian drug king of Panama towered over everyone. Walter was introducing the big man around. Jack studied him. He was handsome in a swarthy way. For such a big man, there was nothing fat about him, except maybe his fingers, which were the size of bananas and looked like they could crush a man's skull with one squeeze.

Walter was nervous. The terror-stricken host and his mammoth guest worked their way through the crowd until they came to Jack.

"Ah, Diego, this is my good friend, Jack Savage. Jack, I would like you to meet Señor Diego Pinzon, one of Panama's foremost businessmen."

Businessman, my ass, Jack thought. He felt drunker by the minute. "How do you do, Señor Pinzon," Jack said as they shook hands. His hand disappeared into the glove of a catcher's mitt.

"Ah, is this the same Jack Savage that had a disagreement with a couple of my friends down at the Balboa Yacht Club recently?"

"If that's what you want to call it, yes, I'm your man, and if those are your friends, I'd hate to see your enemies."

Diego's eyes flashed danger. "I don't like people hurting my friends."

"I know how you feel," Jack said, returning an equally threatening glare. "I don't like people who hurt my friends either. In fact, one of my friend's sons ended up missing when he consorted with a couple of your friends."

They stared at each other with the intensity of two dogs, nose to nose, poised for the first hair to move.

"Well, let's let bygones be bygones." Diego smiled. "We will meet again, sometime. Yes?"

"I hope not," Jack answered.

Both men kept their eyes on each other until the crowd surrounded El Gigante. Jack went back to the bar for another beer. He took a swig and wiped his mouth with the back of his hand. He was getting sloppy. He turned away from the bar and leaned on it with one elbow, the beer bottle in his other hand. The crowd seemed to part for a moment, and to his surprise, he could see Rachel and Diego talking and hugging each other.

Diego grabbed her around the waist and swung her to him, then kissed her. When they broke apart, Rachel was laughing.

Jack kept looking. He was mesmerized by a scene he did not believe. Finally, Rachel and Diego, hand in hand, eased over toward a door. They stood by it for a while, looking around. When it seemed as if they were unnoticed, they slipped into the room, laughing. The door shut quickly. Jack shook his head. He was numb. Why would she do this to him? She didn't have to invite him to this party. Was it just to torture him?

He was really bombed now and held onto the bar to keep it from spinning. Finally, his inebriated brain could take it no longer. He staggered over to the door. His journey seemed to take forever. He tried the doorknob. It was locked. He turned the handle again and again, then started pounding on the door.

One of Diego's thugs grabbed Jack by the shoulder. "The party's over," he said. He strong-armed Jack through the crowd and out of the house.

Jack was too dazed to put up a fight. He had a difficult time finding his car. When he did, he opened the door unsteadily and slid onto the front seat. He fumbled for his keys in his pocket. He was too drunk to even curse. He grabbed the door and shut it, then started groping for his keys again. He stopped and held onto the steering wheel, looking straight ahead. Even as drunk as he was, he felt the pain of embarrassment, rejection, and betrayal. Jack's grip on the wheel slowly loosened, and he drifted down onto the seat.

When Jack awoke, the sun was shining through the windshield onto his face. He dragged himself up to a sitting position using the steering wheel. The pressure in his head felt like it was at least three hundred pounds per square inch. His mouth felt and tasted like it was full of rancid, red snapper scales. He remembered the night before, and his hangover worsened. He looked down the street to Walter's house. Walter's car was gone, but Rachel's car was there. So was another. Jack started his car and drove off. This was going to be one lousy day.

Millie and the Dude had a problem—Zack.

"I just thank God I didn't have any children by him," Millie said.

"That would've made it tough." The Dude knew where this conversation was headed.

"Yes, but I want children. When we first got married, I wanted a child, but Zack wouldn't hear of it. Finally, one day he came home and told me he had gotten a vasectomy. That was it. All the selfish bastard wanted to do was to go drinking and fishing with his buddies."

"Well, I guarantee you there ain't no slash and burn around my balls. I'm loaded for bear. You lookin' out for yourself, Millie? It wouldn't be so great to knock you up while you're still married to numbnuts. I think he'd think there was something fishy." The Dude laughed. They were lounging in the Dude's apartment in Panama City.

"Gimme a break, Nick. I'm not a nurse for nothing. I know a few things about the birds and the bees."

"No sweat, Mil. Just wanna be sure we stay safe until . . . until . . ."

"Until what, oh Great Spearin' Dude?"

"You know."

"Know what?"

"Damnit, Millie, you know damn well what I'm talkin' about."

"Yeah, but I wanna hear it again."

"Until you divorce that fat slob and marry me, and then I'll fill you up so much you'll have all the babies you want. I love you, you sexy bitch."

"That's what I wanted to hear," Millie said as she slipped up on him and did things to him that kept them busy all afternoon.

Jack was miserable. Like a fool, he had let things get out of hand and let a woman emotionally crush his ego. It was all he could do to carry on at work. He no longer heard from Rachel, and he never called her.

Sometimes he thought he would go mad thinking about her, but he held onto his dignity and stayed away from any communication with her.

He couldn't understand why she did what she did. Was she sadistic? Possibly deranged? He knew he would get over her in time, but he couldn't understand why it was so agonizing. They had little in common except for sex. From their first encounter, he thought she was a little strange. Now he knew.

Jack's recreation was working on his boat. He liked being at the shed with Juan and fixing new things on the *Arugaduga*. Juan was a great helper and a wise man to talk to. He had raised five children himself after his wife died giving birth to the son Diego had murdered. There wasn't much Juan didn't know about life, especially the hard parts. Jack confided in Juan, and Juan gave good advice.

"Mistah Jack, doan loose you 'ead ovah woman. She make you kookoo, den fuufuu."

"What the hell does that mean?"

"Kookoo mean crazy, an' fuufuu mean dead, mahn."

CHAPTER EIGHT

I t was a rainy Saturday, and the rain roared on the shed's tin roof for hours. As suddenly as it started, it faded away. Jack was inside the *Arugaduga* installing spear shaft racks. He had made twenty spare, stainless steel spear shafts for future trips. He finally finished the job and stood up in the boat to stretch. When he turned around and looked down, Jack saw a young woman, hands on hips, staring up at him. Her hair was jet black and wildly curly. The face beneath the curls was mischievous, yet intelligent, but most of all, gorgeous.

"What the hell?" Jack said, startled.

"Shake you up?" the young woman said.

"Yeah, a little. What's your name?"

"Tess."

"Tess . . . Tess Delsey? Naw, Tess is a little squirt. Hell, she's in college in the States somewhere."

"Wanna bet?"

"You're Tess Delsey, Paul's little sister?"

"None other."

"Damn. Turn around, turn around."

Tess obliged and made a full turn.

"I'll be damned. College was good to you. You developed a tight little ass, along with an outstanding rest of you."

"I can see you're still the same Jack Savage, foul mouth and all."

"You gonna hold a little honest compliment about you against me?"

Tess laughed. "You haven't changed a bit, nor will you ever. Maybe that's what makes you so charming."

"Why, Tess, is that a proposal of marriage?"

"Oh, man, what an ego. All that diving must have compressed your little pea brain even more."

"That's no way to talk to your elders." Jack was having fun with her but had a strange feeling he would come out the loser in this match. This girl acted smart.

"You're absolutely right. You are quite my senior. I'm really sorry I offended you, sir. I will definitely take into consideration your advanced age in the future."

Jack winced. "Ow, you really think I'm that old?"

"That's the way you talk."

"I've had a lot on my mind lately, and I must admit that when I saw you there, after all these years, I was taken aback by how beautiful a woman you've become," Jack said.

"Am I as appealing as that redhead you've been playing around with?"

"Who the hell told you that?" Jack was serious now.

"Oh, hell, Jack, it's all over town. You know the Canal Zone."

"This is serious shit. Now tell me, how the hell did you find out? Be honest with me."

"It's common knowledge. She meets you here, you go to your house, she takes you to her house. Everyone's talking about it, but you're only going to star for two weeks until someone else takes your infamous place."

"Sonofabitch!"

"What's the big deal?" Tess shrugged her shoulders.

"Ah, you wouldn't understand."

"Try me."

Jack looked at Tess and shook his head. He sat on the edge of the boat, head bent.

"What is it?" Tess climbed the ladder up to him. "You can tell me. I'm Paul Delsey's sister, remember?"

"I appreciate your concern, but it's a little out of order for me to tell you my private life. I'm just pissed that this has gotten around, that's all."

"What, you don't think I know she's a married woman? That she's married to Walter Mendoza, one of the richest men in Panama? That she's—"

"Where the hell did you learn all of this stuff?" Jack ran his fingers through his hair in frustration.

"Somebody must have let the cat out of the bag. I didn't go looking for the info."

"Fuck."

"You're not the only one who's featured in the tabloids this week."

"Oh no, who else is running the gauntlet now?"

"Your crazy-assed friend, The Great Spearin' Dude and Zack Martin's wife, Millie."

"Oh, shit." Jack lowered his head. "Well, you better get out of here before trouble comes your way for just being around me."

"The hell I will," she said.

"Damnit, Tess. You're here with an older man. People will talk."

"Hah, looks like they've already been doing that."

"Yeah, but not about us. Now scoot."

"I will not," she said with her hands on her hips again.

"Do I have to throw you out of here bodily?"

"You wouldn't dare."

"Just watch me," he said as he swung a leg over the side of the boat and started down the ladder.

Tess needed no more encouragement. She was out the door and on her way. She stopped momentarily. "You're gonna need my help someday, Jack Savage," she said, then turned around and walked away.

"Tess, you really do have the nicest little ass," Jack called out to her as he closed the door.

He had not thought about Tess in years. Paul had raised her when their parents had died in a car accident while vacationing in the States. Paul had a good job with the Panama Canal Company and put her through college with his salary and their parents' insurance. From what Jack could see, Paul had been successful raising and educating her.

Jack locked up the shed and went home. He called the Dude. He wanted to warn him before something happened. After an eternity of rings, the Dude answered. "This is none other than The Great Spearin' Dude."

"Can the crap, Dude. We've got a little problem on our hands," Jack said.

"Like what?"

"Like women we're not supposed to be fucking around with."

"What's this got to do with me?" The Dude feigned innocence.

"Do you have to be a flaming asshole all the time? I'll bet the woman in question is there with you right now, if not under you." Jack couldn't control his impatience.

"Okay. So whatta you gonna do, tell the world?"

"Dude, I don't have to. It seems the whole world knows about it already."

"What?"

"I just got it from a good source that you and I have been revealed as the wife stealers of the week with pissed off husbands to go along with it."

"Ah, couldn't be any worse than an eight-foot tiger shark with a spear up its ass."

"Damnit, Dude, will you be serious for once, and listen to me?"

"Okay, okay, I'm all ears."

"You know the crazy broad that I've been mixed up with?"

"How could I forget?"

"You haven't mentioned anything about us, have you?"

"Hell, no. Whatta you take me for? I'm your friend. Why the hell would I do something like that?" The Dude sounded hurt.

"I'm sorry, Nick. I just had to ask. Someone's out there spyin' on us and talking up a storm, and I don't like the shit that's heading our way."

"Chucha madre! Sounds like it's time to get outta Dodge, but it's too late for me. Got too much to hang around for."

"What do you mean?"

"What I mean is Millie's gonna leave that fat, drunk, abusive slob of a husband and marry me."

"Chucha, Dude! You must love trouble. Can't you find enough in the ocean?"

"That's another kind'a trouble. This kind's more dangerous. You'll see."

"Yeah, I'm sure of that. Look, I've got the boat all fixed up for another trip. Are you game?"

"If I can peel Millie off of me, I'm on my way." The Dude laughed and Jack heard Millie laughing in the background.

"Okay, I'll get a hold of Paul and see if he can tear himself away from Polly for a trip. The only thing is that Pete doesn't want to go on any more trips. I'll have to find another driver."

"Go for it Jack, ole' boy, go for it."

Paul's apartment was in the building across the street from Jack's. Tess answered the door.

"What do you want?"

"I just want to talk to Paul."

"What for?"

"Damnit, Tess, that's my business. Are you his guardian, all of a sudden?"

"I ought to wash your mouth out with soap."

"And I ought to give you one hell of a spanking. Now get me Paul."

"Would you spank me very hard?"

"Tess, you're incorrigible." He remembered how Tess was always trying to tag along with him and Paul when she was a kid. They did everything they could to shake her off, but she never gave up trying.

Paul came to the door. When Jack told him he was planning another dive trip to Perlas, Paul didn't hesitate. "Count me in," he said.

"You sure it's okay with Polly?"

"She can spare me for a few days."

"But we don't have a driver anymore. Pete lost his hard-on for the deep blue sea after that last trip."

"Guess I can't blame him, after getting fried alive by lightning."

"Yeah, but we need another driver who's nuttier than a fruit cake and will stay that way no matter what."

"My sister."

"Who?" Jack thought he heard wrong.

"I said my sister, Tess. She's been handling a boat since she was in diapers. And she's not a chicken shit either."

"Yeah, well, she's a girl."

"Tess knows her way around," Paul insisted. "Just try her. She won't disappoint you."

"Man, I don't know."

"What's the big deal? Tess is Delsey-trained. She can handle a boat better than most men. Hell, I've put my life in her hands plenty of times. Don't be such a hard ass. Let her go on the trip."

"For Pete's sake, she's just a kid. Hell, we're going to dive Galera Island. You know what's there. Sharks up the ass, and tiger sharks, too. And if we hit it when that bitch current is there, we'd better have some fancy boat maneuvering or we're gonna end up chopped meat on the reef or shark bait in the deep. Besides, how's she gonna take a piss an' all with us guys around?"

"I'll bring my own bucket," Tess said, coming up behind Paul. "And I'm no kid. I'm twenty-three, not a thirty-six-year-old fart like you."

"You really want to go on this trip with a bunch of foul-mouthed divers like us? You know, your brother's no saint, either."

"I hope not," Tess said. "'Cause if he's become one, he sure raised me wrong."

"So you don't mind hearing us cursing?" Jack smiled. "What if one of us sees that pretty little ass of yours?"

"It's been seen before, by better than any of you."

Jack actually felt a little stab of jealousy. She was beginning to grow on him. "Damnit, if you wanna go that bad, then you're on, but no whining and bitching."

"I'll whine and bitch when I want," Tess said.

Jack threw his hands up in the air. "Chucha madre, Paul. She ever lose a fight?"

"If she'd been a boy she would have beat the shit out of King Kong."

"Well," Jack looked at Tess with a smile, "I'm glad she wasn't a boy."

CHAPTER NINE

Everyone was in high spirits as the trip began. Tess had proven to be a great asset in organizing supplies, buying the food, and check-listing everything, especially radio and emergency equipment. She was better than anyone aboard as a mechanic, be it gas engine or diesel. As a child, she learned about outboard engines from Paul, and she maintained her love for mechanics through adulthood. She even took a few courses in engine maintenance. Tess had never come back to Panama while in college. They didn't have the money for the trip. Instead, she repaired outboard motors each summer at a local shop.

Just as Paul said, Tess turned out to be an excellent driver. Secretly, Jack was glad she was along on the trip. They ran through a few squalls on the way to the islands, and it got a bit rough occasionally, but they finally broke out into visibility and sunshine right where they were supposed to be, heading for the pass between Pedro Gonzales and San José Islands.

"Man, when we get through the pass we oughta hang a right and head for The Monks. Plenty of fish there," the Dude said.

Jack shook his head "Nah, we're heading for Galera Island. We fart around at The Monks, and we'll use up a lot of gas. We'll never dive Galera."

"Just a suggestion." The Dude shrugged. "Where we gonna anchor tonight?"

"Anywhere but near an airfield. Damned if I want to be around when those drug bastards make a delivery from Columbia or wherever they bring that shit in from. Run into an operation like that and people will still be wondering where the hell we disappeared to fifty years from now. I know a nice little anchorage behind a small island that's perfect. The only town anywhere near it is Mafafa, and that's at least ten miles away and around Cocas Point from the anchorage."

"Every time I come down this way, I hear small planes flying all night, no lights, nothing," Paul said.

"Yep, that's them all right, 'cause according to Panamanian law, no small planes are supposed to be flying at night. I don't give a fuck what they're doing, I just don't want to be around when they're doing it. Another thing. There've been some rumors about pirates sneaking up on boats, robbing, stabbing, and one shooting—a Panamanian businessman on his boat for the weekend, right around here."

"Yeah, we all heard about that," Paul said.

"We just have to be on guard at night, that's all. Someone keep an eye open all the time, you know, take shifts." Jack popped open a can of beer. "Hey, Capitana," he called to Tess, who was at the helm. "Want a beer?"

"No thanks, but you could spell me at the wheel for a while."

"Will do." Jack slid onto the large bench next to Tess and took the wheel. "You're doing great, Tess. I'm really glad you came with us."

"Thanks, Jack." Tess looked down and blushed.

"I need you to keep a good eye on us when we're in the water on the back side of Galera. Your brother says you're good and that's good enough for me. I'm just asking you to be extra on the ball when we dive this place. It's not only loaded with sharks, but there's a bitch current that can screw up divers as well as the boat."

"You got it." Tess smiled.

Damn, Jack thought. Tess gets prettier every day.

They arrived just before noon. Galera was shallow on its north side, but around the back, deep rock rivulets ran straight out from the island like rays into deeper water. If there was a strong current and a diver shot a fish, he had to keep it out of these ridges and valleys or the fish would hunker down inside one. The diver would have to swim up current to get back to the fish. This was almost impossible. Shooting a fish in this kind of current on this side of Galera was a good way to lose one's gear or life.

Farther down, the current was another roller coaster ride. A big rock, about two hundred yards off the island, separated deep, shark-infested water from a shallow rock, coral, and barnacle meat grinder on the island side. But there were a lot of fish, and the diving was too good to pass up.

"Been seeing a hellova lotta sea snakes on the surface," the Dude said, pointing to one undulating across the top of the water.

"Yeah, they show up when there's drift in the water. Rarely ever see one when there's no junk floating around," Paul said. "No sweat, though. If one of the little fuckers bites you, you won't have to suffer more than thirty minutes, 'cause death takes over after that."

"Paul," the Dude answered back. "You always say such cheery things. I hope a shark bites one of your ass cheeks." Everyone, even Tess, laughed.

The divers slipped into the water noiselessly. As soon as Jack entered the water, he looked down and saw that the bottom was rushing by too fast. They would have to drift out of the furrowed area before shooting fish. The current was extra strong. With a fish holed up, it would be all a diver could do to hold onto his gun. He saw big snapper everywhere.

"Don't shoot! Don't shoot!" Jack yelled out across the water to the other divers.

Paul knew better, and drifted through the snapper, even though it was tempting to take a shot.

There were sharks darting through the snapper. They weren't aggressive yet but were definitely nervous. There were blacktips, silky sharks, hammerheads, little whitetip reef sharks, bull sharks, and swimming along the bottom, a huge nurse shark. The blacktips were the worse. They weren't that big, about four to eight feet, but they would charge a diver head on, inches from his face mask, turn and head off, then attack again from behind or below. Everything was controllable if the diver kept his cool, but when a big tiger shark came in, chaos followed. The tiger shark didn't care what he ate—fish, garbage, or human.

The Dude knew better but couldn't resist the temptation to shoot a large snapper a few feet away. The clack of his speargun was a chilling warning to the two other divers. Paul and Jack turned toward the sound.

Dumb bastard, Jack thought. He's fucked up the works now.

Paul and Jack fought the current to get to the Dude. As expected, the snapper dove straight down and holed up in one of the deep ravines below, about forty feet down. The Dude was dragging underwater behind the snapper's refuge about thirty feet, caught in the rapid current with most of his line out. Paul arrived on the scene first. He dove down past the Dude and disappeared into the chasm where the snapper was. Jack stayed above him, fighting the current to stay in place.

Suddenly, Paul came out of the rocky furrow with the snapper in tow. Paul had been down a long time, and with the added effort of swimming the current, diving to the bottom and fighting with the fish, he was exhausted. As he drifted along, Jack could see there was something wrong. Paul was fighting with the fish rather than pulling on it. He was tangled, and he was forty feet down. Jack took another quick look at the Dude. He was in as bad a situation. The reel had spun out on him because of the fighting fish and the strong current. His swimsuit and his balls were wrapped tight around the handle and the spool. He was in excruciating pain but couldn't scream for fear of sucking water and drowning.

As Jack turned to face the current, some drifting leaves and twigs hit him, then something larger hit his face mask. It was alive, wriggling and thrashing wildly. A sea snake had drifted into Jack's face mask and had gotten lodged between his head and snorkel. He had to shake the yellow-and-black banded tenant loose quickly. Jack knew one bite to a thin part of his body, especially his ear, meant a nasty death. He did every twist, turn, and dive possible, but the venomous snake was still there. The snake was now fighting for its life, not just trying to get away. As a last desperate maneuver, Jack turned his body with the current and the snake washed off.

If Jack didn't get to Paul and the Dude quickly, they would not only be shark bait but also drowned shark bait. No one ever carried a knife. For some reason, the perfect knife could never be found, and no one could ever find a place to wear one. Strapping to the leg was for hero divers showing off on the beach.

Jack blasted through the surface and looked around for the boat. It wasn't far. Tess was definitely on the ball. Jack waved his gun and yelled. "Tess! Tess! Get over here! Quick! Trouble!"

Tess was there in an instant. "What can I do?"

"Get me a knife! Quick!" Jack threw his loaded gun into the boat.

Tess scrambled around in the boat and came up with a long butcher knife. "It's all I could find." She leaned over the boat and handed it to Jack. He grabbed it and yelled for her to head up to the place where he knew the Dude and Paul were drowning. Jack held onto the boat for the tow. He looked down and could see both of them still struggling. A good sign. At least they were alive.

"Take me upstream of them so I can drift down and cut the lines."

When Tess had taken him far enough up, he let go of the boat and dove to the bottom as fast as his flippers could move him. He only had time for one try. They would be drowned the next time around. There was Paul ahead of him, tangled and struggling with the big snapper. The current slammed them together. Jack grabbed onto whatever he could and started cutting line. Paul began to free himself, but there was just enough line tangled around his leg to hold the fish. Jack crawled down Paul's leg and cut the line to the spear in the bleeding fish. Paul was free, and so was the Dude, even if his balls were in a knot around his Riffe reel. He went for air first, then slowly, painfully untangled his reel. Jack and Paul surfaced not far from him.

In all the excitement, no one took into account the current and where they were heading. It was too late. They were heading past the inside of the big rock. The island side. The shallow meat grinder. The water rushed faster over the jagged shallows. Tess, being so concerned with the divers, was caught in the same raging funnel with the boat. The only thing she could do was lift the engine legs so they wouldn't be smashed. She had to turn off the engines and drift, hoping a coral head wouldn't pop through the hull.

As the divers passed by the shallowest section of the meat grinder, it began to live up to its name. It was like roaring down a mountain stream, but every time they bumped into something, a piece of meat came off. They were slashed in myriad parts of their bodies as they tumbled through the scything wash. Finally they were out and floating in deep water, bleeding.

Paul had lost his gun in the struggle to free the Dude and then himself. Jack's gun was in the boat. The Dude was the only one with a gun, but it had no spear. It was trailing line, and all his attention was riveted to freeing his aching balls from the reel. The line had snagged on a piece of coral momentarily, as he zoomed through the meat grinder, and almost emasculated him.

As they were flushed into the deep on the other side of the rock, there was a welcoming committee waiting for them. It seemed as though every shark in Panama had been aroused by the bleeding snapper, and now the divers were cut bait themselves. Some of their wounds were deep, and the immersion in water kept them bleeding profusely. They looked for the boat, but it was jammed into a coral head, and Tess was doing her best to pole it off with a paddle. There was no time to worry about the boat. Their problem was beneath them. Jack still had his knife, and the Dude finally got his balls back and had the empty speargun for a prod. Jack cut some of the line off the gun and used the rest to tie the knife on the end like a bayonet. They all clustered together on the surface, looking down and facing in different directions.

The blacktips rushed first. They were leery but became bolder with each pass. Jack figured there were at least twenty and a good size since they were in deeper water. He took the gun. The sharks swooped at them inches from their heads, then they started bumping the divers. That was the last maneuver before the bite. A big one rushed Jack from below, mouth open, its teeth bared. As it went for Jack's left leg, he jammed the bayonet deep into its gills. It took off like a rocket, streaming a crimson plume behind it. The other sharks sensed danger and held off their attacks for a while.

"Drowning might have been easier," Paul said, his sense of humor intact.

"You're the next stabber, Aquaman." Jack handed the gun to Paul.

This time, a large ten-foot bull shark made a determined rush. Paul charged the menacing shark and thrust the knife into the top of its head. It pierced deeply, somewhere near its control system. The shark rolled Paul around before he could withdraw the spear, then it continued to roll and spin, out of control down into the deep. Now it was the Dude's turn.

Back at the boat, Tess realized she would have to get out and push the boat off the reef. She knew she was going to get mangled, but there was no other way. She tied her tennis shoes on tightly, grabbed a line, tied it around her waist, and cleated it off on the back of the boat. Then she eased herself off the dive platform into the raging water, guiding herself along the side of the boat, holding onto it as best she could. When she reached the bow where the boat was grounded, she stooped down as far under the boat as possible. Using the strength of her leg and back muscles, she pushed upward with all her adrenalin would allow. It didn't budge. She tried again, with the same results. She put her back to the bow of the boat and her feet on the submerged coral head. She took a deep breath and shoved. The boat moved slightly. She positioned herself the same way again. The results of the next push were miniscule but positive. Tess was running out of steam. Her head was spinning, and she was shaking all over. She braced herself in the same way, making sure her back was square to the bow and her feet firmly planted on the coral head. Like an uncoiling spring, she unleashed all her energy at once with a shattering scream. The boat moved, slowly at first, then easing into the current, it pulled free from its coral prison and picked up speed.

Tess was exhausted now. The line around her waist cinched tightly, and she was jerked off her feet as she was pulled behind the boat. The meat grinder did its job again. Tess was dragged over coral, rock, and barnacle until she could no longer feel the pain of the scrapes and gashes. Doggedly, she handlined herself up to the dive platform. With great effort she hauled herself up onto the structure, then climbed into the boat and untied herself. She ran to the controls to begin lowering the legs of the outboards, but before she did, she checked the water depth. She was in deep water. Down went the lower units. The engines started without a hitch. Tess looked at the deck. It looked like a big fish kill, but the blood was all hers. She could hardly see her legs from the blood. Tess headed in the direction where the three divers would most likely be drifting. She looked up and down, back and forth, for what seemed like hours. She had entered blue water and still no sight of them. Then something caught her eye. It disappeared. There it was again. Gone again. Tess saw it again and recognized it as the fluorescent orange tip of a snorkel. She turned the boat in that direction and gunned the engines.

Things were beginning to get out of hand for the divers. The Dude had the makeshift bayonet now. The sharks were getting bolder and more numerous. The bumpings increased, but the divers punched and kicked back. They were going to take out as many as possible before becoming dinner. A large blacktip shark swooped so close to the Dude, he had to pull back to stab at it. He jammed the bayonet deep into the underside of the predator as it passed by on its side, snapping its mouth. The Dude held onto his gun tightly and was pulled along by the shark. The knife slit the belly of the shark. Its guts rolled out of the cavity and streamed along behind as it fled into the blue. Some of the sharks streaked after it, tearing at its entrails. When the Dude pulled back the makeshift bayonet, the knife was gone.

Suddenly, there were sharks, large and small, streaking past them. They no longer had any interest in the divers but seemed to be fleeing for their lives. The three divers popped their heads out of the water at the same time.

"What the hell's goin' on?" the Dude said, spitting out his snorkel for the moment.

"Don't ask me," Jack said. "But it sure seems creepy."

"Something's coming," Paul said. It was as close to fear as Jack had ever heard in his brave friend's voice. "Something very big."

What came out of the blue gloom of the deep was at first unbelievable, then as reason replaced doubt, terror short-circuited through each diver's body. It was a tiger shark, an old one with a ragged dorsal fin. It was at least twenty-five-feet long and had a mouth as big as a couch. In its mouth was the shark the Dude had just stabbed. The tiger shark shook its head, chomped the smaller shark, then swallowed it.

The three divers popped their heads out of the water for a moment to communicate. "Shit!" Everyone screamed the same word.

"Back in the water! Back in the water! Face the bastard!" Jack said.

Paul had already slipped under. Jack and the Dude were right behind him. They lined up together and watched the freight train of a shark glide past them. It slowly passed, eyeing them with its deadly stare. No one had even imagined a tiger shark could grow that big. A small one was bad, but this monster could inhale all of them at one time.

It circled them from a distance, as if it were curious about these strange things it was going to eat. The divers had to pop up for air occasionally.

Jack and the Dude had snorkels so they could keep an eye on the predator while Paul, who never used a snorkel, gulped air.

What a fuckin' way to go, Jack thought, as the huge shark tightened his circle. The Dude lay on the surface, sucking air through his snorkel, his useless speargun at the ready. Then Paul did something extraordinary. As the shark passed, he rushed it as fast as his flippers would allow. He screamed as loud as he could underwater and punched it with his fist on the side of its head near its gills. The big shark was startled and shot off. It bought them a little time.

Well, if Paul has the balls to fight for his life, so do I, Jack thought. When the big shark came close enough again, Jack swam up to it from an angle as swiftly as possible and punched the killer in the gills, screaming as loudly as he could underwater. It worked, but the shark didn't keep its distance as long as before. The great tiger shark slowly returned, although more cautious this time. As massive as the shark was, it was agile. Using one of its killer tactics, it glided off into the distance until it could barely be discerned, then in a snap, it turned, touching nose to tail, and rushed at the terrified divers.

The Dude was out front with his empty speargun. When the shark seemed about to inhale the three divers, and was close enough to touch, the Dude struck out in a futile effort with the end of his gun. By sheer luck the gunpoint slid down the catfish nose of the big tiger shark and scored a direct hit on its left eye. Eyes were sensitive, even on enormous sharks. The tiger shark shook its head like an animal drying off. It stayed at a good distance for some time, circling, circling, circling.

The divers knew there was nothing in a shark that called for revenge—no feelings of courage or cowardice. It was fight or flight . . . and hunger. The big shark was injured, but it was still hungry. The Dude thought he heard an outboard motor droning sound. "It's Tess!" he screamed, his head out of the water and his arms flailing about in the direction of the approaching boat. He leapt as high out of the water as his flippers would allow. Tess waved back in recognition. The others saw the boat coming but had to keep their eyes on the monster.

"Dude! Quit splashing around! The shark's getting crazy again!" They all went back on alert. The big shark tightened its circles once more.

Suddenly, Tess was there and they grabbed for the dive platform. Paul and the Dude were on the platform and over the transom of the boat like lizards, but Jack was a little farther away. The giant tiger shark was up on the surface now, its ragged dorsal fin slicing through the water. It was going to be close.

Tess grabbed the boom stick, a long aluminum pole with a stainless steel powerhead on the end. It was loaded with 00 buckshot and would go off on contact. The big tiger shark gained on Jack rapidly. The shark's run took it about ten feet from the side of the boat, heading at Jack from the direction of the dive platform. Paul watched, horrified, as his sister leapt from the side of the boat, boom stick in hand like a javelin, and landed in the water almost on top of the monster. There was a muffled explosion with the intensity of a canon that reverberated from beneath the water. Spray shot up around Tess. The killer had lost its appetite at last and brushed by Jack, spinning him in the water. It swam off, trailing blood. Jack helped Tess up onto the dive platform, but she wouldn't get into the boat until he was on the platform and climbed in with her.

Everyone was in shock. They sat on the deck and looked blankly at each other.

"Let's get the hell outta here, Tess," Jack said. He realized he owed his life to her. That was the bravest act he had ever witnessed, and she did it to save his life with complete disregard for her own.

CHAPTER TEN

No one wanted to dive anymore that day, so they pulled up to a white sandy beach in Santelmo Bay on the southern side of Rey Island. They anchored, tended to their wounds, and swam ashore. The Dude and Paul sat on the sand, gulping beer from cans. Tess walked down by the surf, looking for shells. Jack sat by himself on a giant driftwood tree. He looked at Tess, not fifty feet from him. She had an angelic face with high cheekbones and a classic, straight nose of perfect proportions. Tess had the blackest, curliest hair Jack had ever seen, and the way she wore it short, complimented her toned body.

"W'r outta fucking beer," Paul muttered.

"More on th' boat."

"Yeah." Paul remained inert.

"Want me t' get some?"

"Yeah."

"I'm off t' see th' wizard." The Dude laughed, then stood up, staggered down to the water, and swam out to the boat. He was back soon with a diver's net bag full of cold beer.

Jack watched Tess as she walked in and out of the gentle surf, moving some unseen object sideways with her foot or bending down to pick up another small treasure to add to her growing handful. He was amazed at her lithe, athletic beauty and her lovely femininity.

He stood up from his perch on the driftwood log, slapped sand from his swimsuit, and stretched his aching body. Then he walked down the beach toward Tess. She was looking in her hand at the different shells she had collected. The afternoon sun painted and framed her into a glowing masterpiece.

"Whatcha got there?" Jack said with a broad smile.

"Oh, just some shells and coral. They're really unique."

"Let's see," he said.

She held out her hand and showed her find to Jack. He took her hand in his and looked at the shells, feigning interest. It was Tess's hand, and the rest of her, that interested him. Still holding her hand, he looked into her blue eyes and said, "Tess, I want to thank you for saving my life out there today. That was the bravest thing I ever saw anyone do. I just ca—"

"Someone has to look out for you."

"You're one helluva beautiful guardian angel."

She blushed. They looked at each other for a long time before he released her hand. Then they walked down the beach, away from Paul and the Dude, who were now solving all the problems in the world.

"How old did you say you were?"

"I'm an old lady. I'm twenty-three."

"Oh, man. I'm thirteen years older than you."

"So what?"

"Hell, I could be your father. Your grandfather."

"Give me a break." Tess laughed.

"Guess a good-looking gal like you has someone special?"

"To tell the truth, not really."

"Saving yourself for Mister Right, eh?"

"I've had my loves in the past, and even go out on occasion now, but there's this one guy I just can't get out of my mind."

"Do I know the lucky guy?"

"You will, some day." Tess flashed a warm smile.

"Well, I just wanted to thank you for what you did for me. If I can ever be of any help to you, just let me know," he said. Hurt and jealous that he wasn't in Tess's future, he envied the man she couldn't get out of her mind. "Gotta get back to the boat and those two drunks on the beach so we can get into a good anchorage before dark. Don't lag too far behind. Night time comes fast." Jack gave a tight, close-mouthed grin, then turned quickly and headed back down the beach.

With everyone finally aboard, Jack steered the boat to his favorite anchorage behind a small island. The island blocked the wind and the waves and concealed them from any intruders. It rained a hard, tropical deluge with no sign of abating. They ate a damp supper of sloppy chili and drank beer again. The only thing keeping them dry was the ragtop over the center console and that wasn't much. They put plastic tarps over themselves and sat in the rain, drinking and lying to each other.

Tess sat in the driver's seat, mostly out of the rain but shivering from the cold.

Jack saw her discomfort and brought her a tarp. "Wrap up in this and it'll warm you up. Why don't you just go to bed up forward? It's the only dry place on the boat, and it's all yours. You have a nice, soft bunk, and it's comfortable."

"No thanks," she said curtly.

"Suit yourself. We're just gonna stay up all night, drinking beer, getting drunk, and talking and lying about diving and women." Jack felt his beer.

"I've heard that kind of talk before."

"Then you're gonna love this because we ain't even lying yet."

The three divers reveled in their drunkenness, the rain, and stretching the truth. The episode with the giant tiger shark was still fresh in their minds. Nothing they had ever experienced before could match the terror they had felt. They bypassed the subject and kept drinking. The only mention of the event was when Paul bragged about his sister's bravery when she jumped into the water and boomed the shark to save Jack. Then the Dude quickly changed the subject.

"I tell you, Millie's one fine woman," the Dude sighed. "I've banged a million broads, but no one, and I mean, no one, ever laid me like she does. It must be the Panamanian in her. God, but she's sexy . . . with or without clothes."

"Better watch yourself, Dude. Her husband's nuts. He's a cowardly sonofabitch, but they're the most dangerous kind. They'll sneak up behind you and shoot you," Jack said, half seriously and completely drunk.

"Fuck you, Jack. Whattabout 'at damn redhead, Rachel, you been humpin'? She ain't no single gal, an' she's married t' ole Walter."

Tess strained to hear the conversation; their voices didn't carry as far since they were wasted.

"Ah." Jack dismissed everything with a wave of his hand and a turn of his head. "Dude, what else do you know?"

"More'n you."

"Like what?"

"Well I know she's a dangerous, Colombian bitch."

"Colombian? She's from Scotland." Jack became irritated.

"Scotland, my ass. She came from the slums of good ole Cali, Colombia. An', Jack, she's into drugs, big time, an' that makes her very, very dangerous."

"Damnit, Dude, whadaya talkin' about?"

"I tell ya, she's dangerous, man. She's in big with El Gigante."

"What about Walter?"

"Walter's scared shitless. They both have 'im by th' balls. He's just pretendin' t' be a husband. Sure, they're married, all right, but it's El Gigante who's banging 'er. Now it looks like you're humpin' along with 'im. Better watch y'r ass. He's a mean sonofabitch."

Jack leaned back in his sitting position on the deck against the huge fish box doubling as a seat below the steering wheel. Rejected by Tess before he'd even gotten started and lied to by Rachel after she'd sworn she was telling the truth hurt his male ego. His hangover in the morning would be outstanding.

It rained even harder. Paul finally convinced his sister to sleep up forward where it was dry. The others slept in the rain under their ponchos. Jack liked it. The raindrops and the alcohol lulled him to sleep. He dreamed someone was knocking at his door, again and again. He blasted out of the dream into reality, sitting straight up. His eyes darted around in the darkness. It was raining lightly now.

Another boat had bumped into them. Jack reached over and grabbed the gaff from its rack on the gunwale, then quietly slithered on his stomach in the darkness to where he heard the other boat hit. He lay still, waiting. A rope flopped over the stern. Jack got into a low crouch, poised like a jaguar, ready to lunge. His mind raced.

Damnit, he thought. I left my shotgun at home. The flare gun. Where's the flare gun? In the drawer on the center console.

A hand reached over the side of the boat and slipped the rope over the cleat, then grasped the cleat. Jack whipped the gaff down onto the intruder's hand with a crunch. Before the man in the dark could scream out, the gaff whipped upward, catching him in the throat and crushing his larynx in one sizzling smack. He flew backward and landed on the side of his cayuco, a hollowed out log made into a boat. His body balanced for a while, one foot in the water and one in the boat. Then he fell into the boat, flopped, and slid down the rough deck like a dead fish.

Two more men came out of the dark from the narrow cayuco, one behind the other. The one in front had a machete and ran, screaming at

Jack. He tripped on his dead partner but regained his balance and raised the machete again as he leapt on board. He wasn't as fast as Jack, though. As he landed on the stern of the *Arugaduga*, Jack swung the gaff and hit him right across the stomach. The machete-wielding bandito threw his knife into the air and gave a chilling scream. Jack maneuvered the gaff behind him and yanked the hook deeply into the man's back. The bandito jumped around on the stern, held there by the gaff in Jack's hands. Jack thrust the gaff handle forward, sending the man backward and released the gaff, just like a fish. The intruder screamed all the way to the water.

The others were awake now, even Tess. The next boarding pirate was a large, dark man. He jumped aboard, pistol in hand. He walked up to Jack and jammed the barrel of the pistol up under his chin.

Shit, Jack thought, this guy's got two hair triggers, one in his finger and one in his brain.

In one, quick movement the pirate smashed Jack across the side of the head with the barrel of the pistol, and Jack crumpled to the deck. Still conscious, Jack lay motionless, hoping to fool the thieves and buy enough time to devise a plan of rescue.

Paul and the Dude were next. The pirate said something in Spanish and motioned them over to him. He put the pistol up to Paul's head, gave a smile in the dark that showed only his teeth, and clicked the hammer back on the revolver. "Adios, gringo," he said.

Suddenly, a loud explosion followed by a blinding flash came from behind the center console. It rocketed into the big pirate, hitting him in the face with a sizzling smack. The dark man dropped his revolver, screaming as he dug at his eyes and tried to put the flare out. Jack leapt and grabbed the pirate by his legs, lifted him up, and threw him back into his cayuco. The glow of the flare burned brightly as the man writhed in agony on the bottom of his boat.

"Tess, give me the flare gun, quick!" Jack yelled.

Tess rounded the center console and gave Jack the pistol and the cartridges. He loaded the gun and shot a flare into the pirate's outboard engine. The engine exploded. Jack untied the line and kicked the cayuco off into the darkness. "Tess, that was quick thinking, using that flare pistol."

"He was going to kill my brother," she said.

"Okay, you guys, let's pull up anchor and get the hell outta here."

The Dude had the anchor in the boat and locked down, almost before Jack finished his sentence.

CHAPTER ELEVEN

J ack was depressed. The incident with the huge tiger shark gave him bad dreams. The fight with the pirates disturbed him. They had to defend themselves; he had no choice. They were going to be killed. He had never wanted to kill anyone, but he knew he'd do it again if he ever had to fight for his life like that.

But Rachel and Tess bothered him the most. He knew Rachel was no angel. She had been rotten to him at the end of their relationship. He knew she was with Diego, but he was still wildly attracted to her. It was hard to believe what the Dude had said about Rachel doing drugs. But the Dude always had good information. He was rarely wrong.

Why would Rachel lie to him about coming from Scotland? Yeah, she had already lied to him about her boyfriend. And Walter. He was the victim, not her. Ah, hell. She was great in bed, but he had never wanted to marry her.

Not being able to win Tess's heart was even more troubling. He used to chase her away when she was a kid, and now she gave him serious palpitations when he saw her. Even so, he wouldn't get in her way. He lay back on his pillow, murmuring to himself that there were a lot more fish in the ocean and slipped off to sleep.

Still unable to shake off his black mood, Jack went by the shed the next morning to see Juan, who was busy making fishing lures.

"What's up, Juan? I see that nobody's stolen the shed, yet."

"Ah, Mistah Jack. Plenty funny tings 'appen when you gwine, mahn."

"Like, what?"

"Well, you know dat lady wid de red 'air, *pelo rojo*?"

"Yeah, that crazy bitch, Rachel. What of her?"

"She come aroun' 'ere lookin' for you when you gwine, mahn. She no come once, but plenty, plenty tyime. She look coo coo to me, Mistah Jack. She wanna know where you is, an' when you come back. She fright, mistah Jack. She 'ave beeg eye like cow."

"Did she say anything?"

"Only dat she wan speak to you."

"Shit."

"You 'ave troubles, Mistah Jack? Dat lady look like she kyan bring a mahn plenty, plenty troubles."

"Was there anyone else with her?"

"No, she alone."

"Well, if she shows up again, just tell her I'm back. You making any money, Juan?"

"Come dry season I gwine be rich, mahn."

They both laughed.

Jack used to love Friday nights. He'd go over to the Balboa bowling alley and drink Cerveza Balboa draft with his friends. This Friday was different. Jack was too down to go anywhere. He lay in his bed after eating a sparse supper and drifted off to sleep. The knocking woke him up.

He reluctantly got up from his bed and opened the door.

"Rachel, what're you doing here?"

She quickly slid past him into his apartment.

"What the—"

"Close the door! Close the door!" she said, nervously.

"What's going on?"

"I had to see you again."

"Why? What's the big deal? You made your point that it was all over between us," Jack said.

"I'm so sorry for what happened that night. I thought—"

"You thought what?"

"I was trying to protect you. I didn't know that Diego was coming to the party. He's a jealous man and a killer."

"What about that bullshit about you coming from Scotland and that crap about your supposed father and all? You really come from Colombia?"

"Where did you hear all this?"

"I have my sources."

"You don't believe all those rumors, do you?"

"Y'know, Rachel, I sure do."

Rachel walked across the room and sat down on the couch. She bit her lower lip and shook her bowed head. Then she looked up at Jack. "Come over here and sit next to me." She patted the couch.

Damn, but that crazy bitch was gorgeous, Jack thought as he looked at her. He walked over to her, then hesitated.

"Rachel," Jack said. "You have to level with me. No more bullshit. I want the whole, real story. You hear? The real thing."

Rachel nodded.

"So you do come from Colombia?" Jack said. "And you were an orphan?"

"Yes, wasn't I lucky?"

"And that's where you met Diego?"

"Yes."

"What's this Diego Pinzon think about you fooling around on him?"

Rachel stared ahead and didn't answer.

Jack continued. "Hah, I'll bet he'd try to cut my throat if he found out about us."

"Oh, don't get so dramatic."

"You were the one who told me about the necktie parties he gives."

"You're right," she said. "He is a dangerous man, but I tell you, I don't love him, and if it makes you feel any better, I'll make sure he never finds out about us."

"Chucha, if half of Panama and the Canal Zone knows about us, how in hell is he gonna miss it? One thing that really bothers me. Are you dealing and doing drugs with him?"

"I told you, I quit doing that a long time ago."

Again, Jack thought she was lying. He glared at her.

"Oh, come here." She pulled him toward her, put her face close to his, and kissed him.

Jack's will faltered, then collapsed. He picked her up and carried her to his bed. They fumbled with undressing, then lay next to each other. Jack felt like he had a fever, he was so aroused. They both gently stroked each other, trading kisses lightly, fondling. When they couldn't stand the intensity of denial any longer, Jack took Rachel in his arms forcefully. He kissed her hard and she responded, grabbing his strong arms as he pushed her beneath him. Rachel writhed and rocked, squeezing his body with her shapely legs. Jack matched his rhythm to hers, controlling his pleasure until he knew they were cresting the same wave and climaxing became unavoidable.

Early the next morning, Rachel let herself out. Tess, now living in her own place across the street, happened to be downstairs throwing out trash and putting laundry in her washer. She saw Rachel open the screen door of Jack's section of apartments and get into her car.

Zack Martin had heard rumors about his wife's infidelity with the Dude for some time but wasn't completely sure if they were true. Millie had stopped sleeping with him years ago after he had gotten a vasectomy. He had grown accustomed to life in the tropics where the booze was cheap, the sun was shining, and the fish were jumping. After finding out how great the fishing was in Panama, he was gone every weekend, holiday, or day off. He preferred his soused friends' company to his wife's.

The day Zack was served with the divorce papers, he came home after work, got drunk, and waited for Millie. "Where ya been?"

"Late shift at Gorgas." She headed for her room without even looking at him.

"Wait a minute," he said, getting up from his chair. He almost fell over. Millie kept walking toward her room. "I said wait a minute!"

Millie turned and faced him. "What?"

"What th' fuck's this?" He waved the divorce papers in front of her.

"Oh, that's just a copy of my termination as a wife and a mother to all the kids we never had. Also, it says that I will no longer be living with you, so that you can spend more time with your drunken buddies here and out on your booze barge."

"I'm not giving you any divorce. You're gonna stay here 'n be th' wife you ain't been lately." He moved toward her.

"Just keep out of my face, Zack. Go fix yourself another drink and become somebody."

He threw his drink at her. It just missed her head and smashed against the wall behind her. "Damnit!" He lunged for her.

Millie was quick but had no room to move in the small hallway. He tackled her, and she fell backward, smacking her head on the tile floor. Zack punched her in the face again and again, venting his anger and rage while she lay there unconscious. He panicked when she offered no resistance. He called Gorgas hospital and said his wife had fallen, struck her head, and he couldn't revive her.

When the ambulance arrived, the paramedic said, "Hey, man, where did this woman fall from, a plane?" When the medic turned around, Zack was gone. They heard a car start and roar out of the driveway.

Millie was in critical condition with a fractured skull, broken nose and jaw, and a lacerated, bruised, and swollen face. She constantly asked for Nick. One of the nurses called him. The Dude was at the hospital as soon as he could get through Panama City traffic. He saw her in intensive care for just a moment. He couldn't believe it was Millie. She drifted in and out of consciousness. He took her hand and asked her what happened. She wouldn't tell him. He kept asking, until she murmured, "Zack . . . Zack knocked me down." Then she slipped off into unconsciousness again.

Zack was caught in a matter of hours.

Paul and Polly were married in a simple ceremony at the Balboa Union Church. Jack was the best man and Tess was the maid of honor. Polly made a stunning bride, but Tess, dressed in an eggshell blue, full-length dress that brushed the floor when she walked, was so enchanting she took Jack's breath away.

A small reception was held at the Balboa Elks Club after the ceremony. Jack wasn't in a partying mood, so he dismissed himself with a courteous lie. As he walked through and around the dancers, he saw Tess dancing with someone he didn't know and figured it was the guy she couldn't get out of her mind. He passed by them and gave a quick smile and nod to Tess. He walked out the door and into the parking lot to his truck. He heard his name being called. Jack turned around to see Tess running toward him, holding the front of her dress up to keep from tripping on it.

"Where you going?"

"Uh, I've got a lot of stuff to do for work next week."

"C'mon, you can do that later. It's your best friend's wedding party," she said, pulling on his arm.

He jerked his arm away from her grasp. "Sorry, Tess, I'm outta here."

"What the hell's the matter with you?"

Jack could see she was getting fired up. Her hands were on her hips.

"Come right out and tell me! Just tell me why you've been so cool to me, why you've been avoiding me, snubbing me? C'mon, what are you afraid of?"

Her curly, black hair had shaken loose and a thick, black curl fell across her forehead. Jack wanted to grab her and kiss her, but his feelings about her were so mixed that he could only run from her.

"I haven't been avoiding you. I'm not afraid of anything." He lied again. "Anyway, what about your boyfriend in there?"

"Damnit, he's just a friend I went to high school with."

"Ahh." He started to open the door to his truck.

"You wait right here." Tess pointed her finger at him. "Don't you move a damn muscle. I'll be right back." She turned and walked back to the reception.

Jack let out a sigh and leaned on his truck. What the hell was coming now? Why did God have to make women so irresistible? Jack felt the refreshing, cool breeze coming down from Ancon Hill. The clouds floated away, and the stars appeared majestically. Why can't life be simple like that?

Tess materialized out of the darkness. Jack strained his eyes to see what she was carrying. "What do you have there?"

"What's it look like?"

"A bottle? Glasses?"

"Champagne. I stole it from behind the bar. C'mon, let's go."

"And where the hell are we going?"

"Your place. We've got a lot to talk about."

"Like what?"

"Why don't you just shut up and start the damn truck, and let's get the hell out of here." Jack didn't want to fight with her anymore so he drove in silence.

It was only a few blocks to his apartment in Williamson Place. Tess got out first and headed toward the entrance. Jack hesitated by the truck.

"Look, what the hell good is this? I've got my own crazy life. I don't need more problems."

"We're gonna do some serious talking, so let's go," Tess said.

Jack opened the door and let Tess in. As she passed him, he could smell her perfume. It was intoxicating. She popped the champagne and poured some into each glass.

"To Paul," she said and sipped her champagne glass dry. Jack followed suit. Tess filled the glasses again. "To Polly." They both emptied their glasses again.

"Wait, wait," Jack said. "What're you trying to prove?"

Tess swiped the glass out of his hand and filled them both again. Jack was beginning to feel the effects of the alcohol.

"This is getting a little outta hand. What's the reason?"

"Drink up, lover boy, this one's for your flaming redhead."

"Damn you," he said, and slugged it down sloppily. Half of it spilled on his shirt.

Tess laughed. "Guess we better take a break."

"What's the matter? Can't take it?"

Tess poured another two. They drank again. This time it was enough. They both walked a bit unsteadily over to the couch and sat down.

"Now, what's this we have to talk about?"

Tess was high. "All cursing and name calling aside, what do you think of me?"

"Do we have to do this? Why don't we just forget this crap and part company? Hell, you're Paul's little sister. It was the champagne I drank at the reception. I was loaded when I left. That's why I left. You're a woman that any man would be lucky to have."

"Yes, we have to do this. I want to know why you're treating me like a pariah. What turned you off that day on the beach, down at the Perlas?"

Tess sat across from Jack on the couch. She stared straight at him, looking for an answer. Jack let out a sigh; he wouldn't meet her eyes. He pursed his lips, bit his lower one, then turned to Tess. He stared at her lovely face for a while before he spoke.

"I'm grateful for what you've done for me. I'd be shark shit on the bottom of the ocean floor if it hadn't been for you. You saved us again, with that flare pistol, when those pirates boarded our boat."

"You don't owe me a thing for that."

"Will you let me finish?"

Tess was quiet.

"Okay, now where were we?" Jack felt lightheaded. "Oh, yes, now I remember. Earlier, on the beach, yes. I was looking at you walking in the surf, with the sun on you, and realized how beautiful you really were, in every way, everything a man could want. So, I . . . I thought that maybe, you and I . . . the both of us . . . that is . . . I thought, maybe we could get together. Well, damnit, I wanted to get to know you better, like more than just diving and fishing, but you got this other guy you said you can't get out of your mind. I guess I got childish and let my feelings get hurt." Jack avoided Tess's eyes.

She put a hand on his arm. "Couldn't you tell how I felt about you? Couldn't you see that all these years I've wanted to be with you? You rarely gave me the time of day. You never gave me any indication that you even liked me. Everything you ever said to me was either smart-assed or vile. You were always unavailable, or I was too young. And now, you sanctimonious bastard, you're sleeping with that redheaded, Colombian bitch, who's married to one of your friends. What a nice guy you are, so don't tell me about getting your little feelings hurt." The champagne affected her speech. "You are such a dumb ass."

"I had no idea that you felt that way about me. What about the guy who you can't get out of your mind?"

"You damn fool. If you can't figure out that one, you're dumber than you look."

"Why didn't you tell me?"

"Do you really think it would have made any difference? I didn't think you cared."

Tess stood up and weaved unsteadily on her feet. She tripped and fell, laughing. Jack helped her up.

"I'll take you home," he said, soothingly.

"To hell with you," she said, shaking off his hands. "I can get home on my own. Don't need no old bachelor's help."

She fell again, and when Jack picked her up this time, her face was green. He rushed her to the bathroom just in time.

Jack got a wash rag and cleaned up her mouth and face, and the few spots on her dress. Then he picked her up, marveling at how light she was, and put her into his bed. He undressed her to her slip and tucked her in. He went to sleep on the couch.

The next morning, Jack was making coffee and toast when Tess rolled out of bed at eleven o'clock. She walked into the kitchen in her slip, with her hand on her head. "You got an aspirin or something?"

"Coming right up," Jack said, cheerfully. He disappeared into the bathroom, returning with two tablets in his hand. He gave them to Tess and got a glass of water. She downed them. "How're you feeling?"

"Like I'm going to die." She put both hands to her temples and moaned.

"Why don't you lie down in my bed for a few hours until your headache goes away? Then you can get dressed and I'll take you back to your apartment."

"No, I'll get dressed and go now."

"I'll drive you home."

"No, I can walk. It's only a few buildings down."

"C'mon, it'll save you the trouble of walking in your long dress, feeling lousy."

"I said no!"

"Fine, fine. It's your call. Go."

Tess walked into Jack's room and slammed the door. Jack fixed himself a cup of coffee. Eventually, the door to his room burst open and Tess stormed out.

"Want a cup of coffee?" Jack asked.

Tess rushed past him in her rumpled dress. At the door, she turned around. "When it comes to women, you're an idiot. You don't know how to talk to a woman. You don't know how to use the words she needs to hear." She walked out, leaving the door open behind her.

What the hell did I do? Jack shook his head.

Tess became completely unavailable to Jack. She hung up on him when he called, and when he saw her in public, she acted as if he didn't exist. Eventually he began seeing her in the company of other men. She seemed quite happy. Jack felt like someone had run a sword through his stomach every time he saw her with someone else. About a month later, Paul called.

"What'd you do to my sister?"

"I didn't do anything to her. You know I wouldn't harm Tess . . . ever."

"Well, something's got her going. I've never seen her so worked up before."

"Ah, maybe I said something to her at the reception, when I was drunk. I don't know. Maybe she's still upset about that hairy trip we had down at the islands."

"I don't think so, but if you find out what's eating her, let me know, will you? She's getting to be a big pain in the ass."

CHAPTER TWELVE

Now that Zack was out of the picture, the Dude and Millie spent a lot of time together. Everything was going well except when Millie would ask the Dude if he ever intended to get a regular job.

"Is that your condition for staying with me? Do I have to dance to your tune of employment?"

"Of course not, I just thought that if we have any future together, we have to keep our heads above water, that's all."

"I've done damn well at keeping my head above water for a long time, and I'm not talking just about diving. Why the hell do you keep bringing up that subject?"

"Nick, do you love me?"

"What kinda question is that? Don't I always tell you I do?"

"Yes, but I mean do you really love me? More than just the sex and the fooling around."

"What are you getting at? Whaddaya want me to do? I don't like steady jobs, but I always make money selling marine supplies and dealing in the fish market. What's the big deal?"

"Oh, so that's it," Millie said. "It's not a big deal, huh?"

"Chucha madre!" Dude flared back. "What the hell's the matter with you?"

"Most real men have a job."

"What?" The Dude was shocked. "When have I ever been cheap? When have I ever neglected you?"

"Just a thought." Millie looked at him.

"I guess Zack was a real man," the Dude said.

"If that's the way you want to look at it." Millie straightened up, adjusted her purse strap over her shoulder, and prepared to leave.

"Wait, before you go. Why is this money thing so important to you?"

"Oh, Nick, you're going to spend your whole life playing. Well, I can't play anymore. I have to work for a living."

The Dude grabbed her by the shoulders. "Let's get married."

"I'm not getting married under these conditions."

"Whaddaya mean?"

"Just that. I'm not getting married because we had an argument."

"Damn it, I was gonna ask you anyhow, and I was gonna do it today, too. So don't give me any of this crap."

"Crap? So it's crap, you say? Well, Mister Great Spearin' Dude, you haven't found out the meaning of the word crap yet." She turned around quickly and walked away.

Paul and Polly couldn't have been happier. They both had good jobs but couldn't afford proper housing yet. The apartment they lived in was built in a hurry. No attempt was made to cover up any construction necessities like pipes, beams, planking, or electrical fixtures. They didn't have the seniority in their government jobs to rate a better house but that would come later. In the meantime, they enjoyed their little apartment together in Williamson Place, where most newcomers started out. They would have been happy in a leaky shack, as long as they had each other. There was one problem, though. Tess.

"Damnit, Tess, what the hell's the matter with you? You're no fun anymore. All you do when you come around here is bitch, bitch, bitch. God, we used to have fun all the time, but now you're nothing but a pickle ass. If you hate that fuckin' Jack Savage so much, I'll give you my speargun and you can walk over to his apartment and put a spear through him."

"I'd like to," she said. "As for being a bitch, well I'll do you the favor of not darkening your doorstep with my pickled ass from now on." She headed for the door.

"Wait, wait," Polly said. "Don't go. Please. I think I know what you're going through. I know because I've gone through a similar situation with 'you know who.' Let's talk. I know I can help you."

Tess hesitated.

"Paul, why don't you go out for a while?"

"But, I—"

"Paul." Polly gave him the look.

Paul left the apartment without arguing.

"Everything I do seems to be wrong. I always say the wrong thing. I always scare Jack away." Tess sat at one end of the small dining table, resting her elbows on the table, her face in the palms of her hands.

"Do you think Jack cares for you?"

Tess sighed loudly. "I don't know. When I lost my mom, I didn't have anyone to talk to except Paul. And he wasn't helpful with much. How do you know if a guy likes you or not?"

"Oh, there're lots of ways."

"Like what?"

"Has he ever told you how pretty you are? Has he ever said you were someone special? Does he ever seem to act jealous over you? When you're with him, does he seem tense or excited?"

"Well, kinda . . . yeah. I guess he's sorta done all that. I'm the one who told him that I love him."

"What was his response?"

"He tried to tell me that he cared for me the same way, and all that, but the bastard irritated the hell out of me with all his jelly-spined reasons for not telling me before. I didn't believe him. It pissed me off, big time."

"So what did you do?"

"Well, I was drunk that night." Tess told her about the night at Jack's house and the next morning. She told Polly how she had treated Jack the past few weeks. "Then he starts shacking up with that bitch redhead, Rachel, again. I could kill his miserable ass."

"Whoa, girl. Slow down." Polly held up her hands. "Am I allowed to offer some constructive criticism?"

Tess nodded.

"You're not going to get a man by torturing him. Granted, a little bit of torture is necessary, but you've got to know when to stop. If you play hard to get too much, too long, he'll assume that you're really not interested in him and you'll soon see him with someone else. You have to be out of his grasp just long enough for him to lunge into yours. As far as jealousy is concerned, never let him see that green spark in your eye . . . until you've captured the sonofabitch." Both women laughed.

"But what am I going to do now?"

"I have a feeling that Rachel is not the kind of woman that Jack wants to settle down with. Besides, she's married, and I understand she runs around with a pretty fast crowd. This may be something you have to ride out for a while, but in the meantime, let's see if we can change your approach. Jack Savage is about to tangle with the most irresistible woman he'll ever meet."

Jack knew it was wrong, but he called Rachel. She was still crazy, but he was still wildly attracted to her. It wasn't the same way he felt about Tess, but Tess had made it clear she didn't want anything to do with him. Soon he was seeing and sleeping with Rachel regularly.

They were getting careless about their meeting times, places, and where she parked her car. Their encounters were pure sex. It was as if they were both satisfying an unquenchable, carnal lust, using each other's bodies. As soon as they were behind closed doors, they were all over each other. Sex with her was uninhibited, and Jack lost himself in the pleasure.

Although Jack was afraid Diego Pinzon had all the details of Rachel's dalliances with him, it didn't stop him from seeing her. No matter what Rachel said about Diego having other women and not caring for her, Jack knew Diego would consider her his property. He would want revenge. But when Jack was in bed with Rachel, he forgot all about Diego.

One Friday night, Rachel drove to Jack's apartment and walked up the stairs to his door. She didn't even have to knock—Jack was waiting for her. She fell into his arms, laughing. He closed the door, undressing her as he kissed her. They made it to the kitchen floor when there was a knock on the door.

"Who the hell could that be?" Jack said. "Just a minute!"

They put their clothes back on and Jack unlocked the door. It was as if a waterfall had descended upon him. Two men rushed him with a third one behind them. They bowled Jack over, lashing out at him with lead-filled, leather blackjacks.

"Enough!" The booming voice belonged to Diego.

Jack lay on the floor, bleeding from cuts all over his head and face. He fought to stay awake. Rachel had retreated to a corner of the small kitchen, her eyes wide with terror as she pressed herself against the wall.

"So, Jack Savage, you like to play with another man's woman, eh? Not very smart, no, not very smart at all. You know how jealous men are of their women." Diego leaned over Jack as he spoke.

Jack could barely focus on the face above him. He tried to speak but couldn't form any words. His right arm was numb, and he was bleeding from his nose and mouth.

Diego reached down and grabbed Jack's shirt by the collar. He yanked him up off the floor and thrust his face into Jack's. "You have anything to do with Rachel again, and I will kill you. Do you understand?" Then he shoved him backward. Jack's head hit the floor with a sickening smack. Diego grabbed Rachel's arm and yanked her through the doorway, followed by his two men. "No more romancing on the side for you, my dear."

Jack regained his senses when he saw the three men drag Rachel down the stairs. He had an amazing constitution and a secret weapon—anger. With all the strength he could muster, he got to his feet and staggered to the door. He could hear the men struggling with Rachel on the stairs. Jack grabbed a brass flower pot by the handle and headed for the stairwell. The men were too busy with Rachel to notice Jack's approach. Jack dove down the stairway at the two men in back of Diego and Rachel. He toppled one with his plummeting body while in the same motion hit the other man with the heavy flower pot. The one he hit with his body flew down the stairs into Diego and Rachel, who also tumbled down the stairs. The victim of the flower pot never knew what hit him. He was unconscious.

Jack's rage made him immune to pain. He leaped on Diego, swinging his arms. The force of his flying body, coupled with a vicious punch, knocked Diego down the rest of the stairs and plunged him through the heavy, wooden screen door.

"Rachel, get into your car and get out of here!" Jack yelled at her, shoving her through the destroyed door. Diego was getting up fast. Jack ran Rachel to her car. He helped her in and she nervously started it up. "Go! Go!" She took off.

As Jack turned around, a blackjack smacked him across the side of the face. Diego stood over him, slapping the weapon against his palm. "Now, Jack Savage, you're going to get the beating of your life." Diego knelt down next to Jack's head and raised the blackjack high above him. As his body flexed to bring down the killing blow, he landed on his victim.

"You move one muscle, and I'll beat you to death," Tess said, wielding a shovel.

Diego was completely dazed from the smack on the head that Tess had given him.

"C'mon, Jack, let's get out of here." Tess helped him to his feet.

With his arm over her shoulder and hers around his waist, they weaved their way to her apartment. She laid him down in her bed and cleaned him up, tending to his wounds. She called the Canal Zone police and told them where the bodies were. The cops got the two men but Diego was gone.

"If I had a gun, I would have blown him away."

"Tess, are you going to spend your whole life saving mine?"

"You know, I think I am. I'm no Rachel, I'm true to my man, and by God, he'd better be true to me."

It wasn't that difficult a decision for Jack to make. He really did love her.

CHAPTER THIRTEEN

"Hey, what the hell did you do to my sister? She's been the sweetest gal that Polly and I have ever seen." Paul had caught up to Jack walking home from work one afternoon.

"Oh, we just talked things out a little, that's all."

"Must have been one helluva talk."

"Hey, Paul, I've got an idea in mind that I've been thinking about for a long time now."

"Oh, God, not again."

"Well, it's really crazy, and you're gonna think I'm nuts when I tell you."

"I already know you're wacko, so what's this new way you've found out to try to kill us again?"

"You know how those big dorado swim around the shrimp boats when they're culling their catch and shoving the trash fish out the scuppers, and how the dorado go wild, like piranhas, eating them?"

"Yeah."

"Let's dive it. We don't have to shoot anything, just see what it looks like down there with all those fish going wild. I got a Nikonos underwater camera. Get some great shots."

"You are one fucked-up, crazy sonofabitch. You know what's swimming around down there with those fish?"

"Yeah, there's a shark here or there."

"Here or there? You can walk on the bastards."

"Yeah, well . . . you don't think they'd bite you, do you?"

"Oh, hell no. They're the toothless kind."

"Ah, come on, quit kidding around."

"No, you quit kidding around."

"Let's just head on down to the islands and find a shrimp boat, let me do my thing, then we can go regular diving for the rest of the weekend."

"Hell, why not?"

"I'll get the Dude, too."

"Yeah, maybe some shark'll do the world a favor and convert his worthless butt into shark shit." Paul smiled.

"C'mon, man, you don't hate the Dude, do you?"

"Nah, he can't help it if he's a moron."

"You know he's a good diver, and you gotta admit, he always makes us laugh."

"Yeah, but he really does a great job of almost killing us every time we go out."

"Then what would we have to talk about after the trip? Oh, yes, we shot a few snappers and groupers. Anything else happen? No. Remember, no bad trip, no good story."

Jack and Paul laughed.

"Oh, Paul, another thing. Could you tell Tess she won't be coming along as driver?"

"Ha! You tell her. She hears you aren't taking her as driver and she'll be meaner than a bull terrier. Why don't you want her along?"

"I . . . I just don't want anything to happen to her, that's all."

"What're you hiding? Why all this sudden concern for my sister?"

"Nothing . . . nothing, really. I . . . I just, well, you know . . . I . . . uh . . ."

"Ah, so now I see. You and Tess got something going on between you two. You banging my sister?"

"Hell, no. Anyway, she's a big girl now. She can talk for herself."

"Your lives are you own. I'd be proud to have you for my brother-in-law." Paul slapped Jack on the back.

The Dude was ready as always. Tess was the driver. Jack couldn't say no to her. She was on her summer vacation from teaching second graders—two months free until school started again. They were underway before sunup. As usual, the Dude jumped around with more energy than everyone combined. It had become light when they approached their first shrimper. They waved to the crew and got return waves, laughs, and dirty chuckles when they saw Tess in her shorts.

Jack loaded a gun with a short line and a spear shaft with no point. He didn't care to shoot anything but brought the speargun in case of a shark attack. Without the detachable spearpoint, the shaft wouldn't stick, just a mean jab and a quick retrieve by the short line for instant reloading.

"Well," he grinned, "nothing like a damn fool for a damn fool venture." he slid over the side into a sea full of iridescent, blue-green dorado crowding around the shrimp boat, waiting for the next dump of scrap fish.

Jack saw thousands of dorado swimming all over the place. Bonito, the small, red meat tuna, clustered below and flared occasionally when sharks made intermittent passes at their school. Jack raised his head out of the water, spit his snorkel out of his mouth, and called to the boat that was floating along about thirty feet from him. "It's fantastic! The colors and the amount of fish are remarkable!"

"See any sharks?" the Dude called back.

"Couple of little ones. Come on, pick me up and take me back to the shrimper."

The shrimp boat moved along at a steady, slow pace, dragging two nets, one on either side of the boat. The doors of the net cut through the water, sliding to the sides and down to the bottom. The diving wooden doors would open up to catch the shrimp along the bottom. They pulled in a test net every hour and the big nets about every four to six hours. Tess maneuvered the boat to Jack so he could climb in. She motored up to the bow of the shrimper where he would drop in again. They did this again and again for as long as Jack dove by the shrimp boat. Jack wouldn't be able to keep up with the shrimper by swimming.

He began to slide into the water when Tess said, trying to keep her voice as quiet as possible, "Jack, please be careful, and don't do this much. I've got a bad feeling." She put her hand on his shoulder and squeezed it lovingly. He grabbed her hand and returned the gesture. Then he was back in the water.

The view was magnificent. Large four- and five-foot dorado swarmed him. Bonito swam all over and around. Small jacks clung to the underside of the hull of the shrimp boat for fear of getting gobbled, which many of them did. Jack drifted back toward the stern of the shrimper. Then he saw the sharks. More than he could count. First it was the blacktips, from four to seven feet in length. They lunged at him from every direction. They were like dogs protecting their turf, testing the intruder. They attacked his face, turning off at the last second, only to reappear beneath him, coming up from below to run up the length of his body, snapping their wicked jaws.

Jack considered shooting one of them but didn't know if there were larger sharks around that would be attracted by the vibrations of a wounded shark. His decision not to shoot proved wise. A large shark slid out of the hazy depth below and cruised in Jack's direction. It swam up to him, almost touching nose to face mask, turned and swam back down into the murk. Jack shook all over. The game wasn't fun anymore.

Jack had drifted too far back behind the shrimp boat into shark country. He signaled for the boat to pick him up. Tess pushed the throttles down hard and raced toward him. She wasn't quick enough. A huge hammerhead shark appeared on the surface behind Jack. The shark's massive, pointed dorsal fin reached so high out of the water it flopped over to one side slightly. Its hammerhead looked like it was six feet across, and it had eyeballs the size of baseballs.

Everyone in the boat screamed and pointed behind Jack, but Jack's head was in the water. He was breathing through his snorkel and couldn't hear them. The shark bumped him hard from behind. He was pushed forward with his head whiplashing backward. Immediately he rolled over the living platform and dropped below the surface.

Jack trembled at the size of the monster. The shark seemed more curious than aggressive, but Jack knew this fish could snap him in two. The shark circled him, becoming increasingly agitated with each pass. Jack had his speargun ready. At one time, the big shark's eyeballs were close enough to poke with his gun. Jack waited for the giant head to slip by, then jabbed it in the gills. With one spontaneous shudder of its body, it was gone. Jack grabbed the side of the boat and slid into it.

"That was like Galera!" he said as he thudded onto the deck. He babbled on, reliving the tiger shark experience off Galera Island.

Tess was all over him, holding and comforting him. He eventually recovered his senses but stayed in Tess's nurturing arms. Paul took the wheel and headed for the Perlas Islands.

"Hey, you guys," Jack said, when he'd finally revived, "since we've got some time, how's about heading for Isla Casaya and do a little pearl diving? Great shells, the meat's delicious, and who knows, someone might get lucky and find a pearl. What say?"

"Let's go diving," the Dude said.

"Dude," Paul said, "you're always putting the glums on everything." Paul couldn't resist any chance to irk the Dude.

"Let's look for pearls," Tess joined in.

Within an hour they were floating over the pearl oyster beds off Casaya. Before they could jump in the water, Paul started one of his lectures. The Dude slapped his forehead.

"The pearl oyster is difficult to find unless you know what to look for," he said.

"Oh, no." The Dude was almost out of the boat.

Paul ignored him. "The pearl oyster likes an environment of sand and rock, preferably in sand between two rocks, where its hairlike roots fasten to, and between, the rock or rocks. It also prefers an environment where there is sufficient current to bring food to it. The giveaway is the open mouth of the oyster as it feeds by ingesting miniscule organisms that float through its gaping shell orifice."

"Done yet?" The Dude was almost in the water.

"Not yet," Paul said. "The opening resembles a black, wavy line from above. They are usually found from fifteen to sixty feet in depth." Everyone was in the water.

"To pull the oyster out, you have to grab the shell by the sides and rock it back and forth, end to end, until you rip it free of those hairlike roots that anchor it to the rock."

By the time he'd finished, everyone was busy putting oysters into buckets to check them for possible pearls. Pearls were far and few between so the competition was fierce. Even Tess was in the water competing for the most oysters. After they'd had enough of diving for oysters, they crouched in the boat and shucked their catch. They were careful to check all the meat around the mantle and any other fleshy parts of the oyster for the hard lump that could be a pearl.

The Dude found a small white pearl about the size of an enlarged match head. He let out a howl, then got back to shucking oysters. Paul lucked out with an even larger one that was twisted and gnarled, but it made him happy.

Tess found nothing and put all her oyster meat in the community pot.

"Well, at least I'm not alone. I've got empty-handed Jack here with me." She smiled at Jack.

Jack returned the smile from his squatting position over his oyster pile. He was down to his last few. He picked up a fairly large one he had found on his deepest dive. He remembered it because it had a gouge across its shell. He inserted his knife into the right place, cutting the muscle that held the oyster shut. As he ran his fingers through the oyster's mantle and surrounding flesh, he felt a large, marble-like lump. He moved aside the flesh covering the mysterious lump and looked down at the most exceptional, iridescent, deep blue pearl he had ever seen. It was about the size of his little fingernail and almost a perfect oval in shape. He quickly slipped the pearl into the small pocket of his swimsuit and zipped it up. He told no one about his find.

They shot a few small fish to go along with Tess's oyster stew, and with cold beer, everyone enjoyed the wonderful lunch.

"Y'know, we should have picked up some of those scallops that were scurrying around there on the bottom. They would have been great in the stew," the Dude said.

"You ever try cleaning them? It takes an hour to get a cupful," Paul said.

"Hah, I wonder how all those bastards out in their cayucos clean theirs," the Dude said.

"They don't. They sell them to the Japanese who're anchored off Catalina Rock about five miles. The Japs have their own processing plant aboard. They eat everything but the shell, and I think they use the shell for something, too."

"Y'know, I've never seen so many scallops in my life," the Dude said.

"It's a cyclic phenomenon," Paul said. "Every ten or so years the scallops come from God knows where and swarm the shallows. I only remember it happening once before."

"Yeah, look at all the shacks the hoochers've built on all these islands, especially Bolanos, because of those damn scallops. The sonsabitches've ruined all the islands in the area. Where the hell'd they all come from? Where'd the fuckers get all the money to buy those new outboard engines, boats, an' all the scalloping nets and gear?"

"Y'know, Dude, for once I agree with you. It seems like every bastard in Panama is out there trying to make a buck and fucking up the environment in the meantime. It doesn't bother me a bit to see fishermen making their living, but a lot of these guys are cutthroats, killers, and pirates. Hope you brought Pomeroy, Jack. Not looking forward to going through another night like that one after we dove Galera about a year ago."

"Pomeroy's asleep now, up forward in Tess's quarters, and believe me, he's loaded and ready with some special shot in him. It'll be a poor man that eyeballs him when he spits."

"They can't all be cutthroats. I've seen some of those poor men begging for water. That's terrible to see someone beg for water," Tess said.

"We'll give them all the water we can spare, and a few beers to a couple of them, but we'd be out of everything in a minute if we didn't turn our heads when we had to. Really, it shows how careless they are. Water and gasoline are number one out here," Jack said.

"I know, I know, but it still breaks my heart to see them."

Jack drew her close and rubbed her shoulders.

"So, where we gonna anchor tonight, admiral?" Tess saluted Jack.

"How about up by Mogo Mogo? Anyone have any objections?" There were none, so they headed north.

Tess motored the *Arugaduga* three miles to Mogo Mogo Island and a small anchorage. For the men, sleeping conditions were the deck and a plastic tablecloth over them for warmth and rain protection. Tess would sleep forward. When she complained that it was sissy, Jack told her until she was properly married, she would sleep up there alone.

"You got anyone in mind?" she asked him.

"I'm no matchmaker, but I think I could dig someone up."

Tess flipped him the bird.

"How did you learn such a nasty sign?" Jack said in feigned shock. "Do you know what that means?"

"Well, I think it means fuck you, Jack." Everyone laughed.

"Arghh. You got me, you got me." Jack grabbed his throat and crossed his eyes. In a flash, he grabbed Tess's head and kissed her quickly on the mouth.

"Hey! You just kissed my sister," Paul said.

"That's right." The Dude backed him up. "No messin' around with the crew."

Tess stood up and put her hands on her hips. "Yeah, how dare you. You have some nerve, Jack Savage." Tess closed in on him, eyeball to eyeball. "How dare you kiss me for such a short time." She grabbed him around the neck, stood on her toes, and pulled his head down to hers, for a long, loving kiss.

Tess turned to her brother and said, "Did you know?"

"I knew, I knew. Go easy on my sister, Jack, or I'll spear you, I swear."

"She will get nothing but my utmost respect. Anyway, you're always gonna spear someone. When are you going to spear the Dude?"

"In due time. In due time," Paul said.

They began to get things in order to retire for the night, when two men in a small cayuco paddled up to them just before dark. They had a bag of marijuana to sell.

"Chucha!" the Dude said. "We could buy the whole bag for five bucks, man. Smoke ourselves to Jupiter."

"Tell 'em thanks, but no thanks. We don't need that shit. Anyway, look at how they're casing this boat. Hell, they know everything we have aboard by now except Pomeroy." Jack shook his hand in a firm "no" signal to the two natives. They began to pull away.

"Jack, a little bit of the weed is good for you, man. Besides, they're from Casaya. They're good people. We know 'em all."

"First of all, a little bit of the weed isn't good for you. It makes you a lethargic, dopey, walking dead. We need to be alert tonight. Second, I don't recognize either of those bastards from the village of Casaya.

Look at all those scallopers' squatters shacks on the other end of Casaya. Those two might have come from the Island of Casaya, but they sure as hell weren't from the town. And third, did you see how they were giving this boat the once-over with their beady little rat eyes? I'm serious, expect unwelcome guests tonight. They are on their way, right now, to tell their party-crashing cronies how much shit those rich gringos have in their boat. Have you any idea what your choice of weapons will be when 'Hail, Hail the Gang's All Here' starts tonight in the rain?"

"Aww, Jack, you ain't serious, are you?"

"Dude, you think I'm serious about this girl?" Jack had his arm around Tess.

"Looks so."

"That's how serious I am about this situation."

"Well, why don't we move?"

"To where? The cocksuckers are everywhere, and anyway, I'm not moving. Since the war in El Salvador is still going on, and Noriega is in charge here in Panama, I never anchor anywhere near an airfield on these islands. Remember those planes I told you about? It wouldn't be a nice feeling to anchor beneath a runway when a drug or gun-running plane landed. A big honcho could pull up next to us to pick up his cargo. Hell, they wouldn't have any choice but to grease our asses. No witnesses. They would simply claim that we must have been lost at sea."

"Those aren't the guys I'm worrying about," Paul said. "It's the little bastard that works a mom-and-pop outfit. He has his drugs stashed, and his weapons, mostly AK-47 automatic assault rifles, heading for Salvador, Panama, or God knows where. The little prick's been saving up his stash, and the one thing he wants and needs, more than anything, is a nice fast boat. Kinda like what we got. Isn't that a coincidence?"

"Don't worry, I've got a wonderful surprise for 'em besides Pomeroy," Jack said.

"I hope so."

"Lighten up, Dude," Paul said. "Hang a good one on with a few more beers and just imagine what you can do. If you can stand up to a twenty-five-foot tiger shark, you certainly can stand up to a five-and-a-half-foot man." This was probably the first compliment Paul had ever given the Dude.

"Yeah, I guess you're right," the Dude nodded. "I'd still like ta throw a few of those pricks to that ragged-finned bastard."

"Hey, that's a great name for that shark." Tess laughed. "Ol' Rag Fin."

"So be it, my beauty, Ol' Rag Fin it is," Jack said, rolling one of her black curls around his finger.

It began to rain lightly, almost a mist. Jack had some lumina lights. He snapped and shook them, and the phosphorus inside glowed a lime green, easing the complete darkness. They kept the lights on the deck so no one could see them from outside. Jack and Tess sat close to each other under Jack's plastic tablecloth to keep out the rain. The Dude and Paul sat in the sprinkle without their covers. Beer and conversation flowed. After two beers, Tess excused herself to go to sleep. She gave Jack a big kiss, which he generously returned.

"Tess," Jack said as she climbed into her bunk, "you know where Pomeroy is, don't you? And the flare pistol?"

"You bet," she said, "and all the ammo for both of them."

"Okay, now pass me that plastic bag there."

"What's in it?"

"Tuna bombs."

"What's a tuna bomb?"

"I'll explain later, just pass the bag and give me a kiss."

She kissed him tenderly. "Jack, why don't you sleep up here?"

"Two reasons. One, I wouldn't be able to keep my hands off of you and something would happen."

"I wouldn't mind."

"Two, Paul would spear me." Jack backed out of the forward cabin, laughing.

The rain came down harder and everyone huddled under their plastic tablecloths. Jack worked beneath his. He had a small container of gasoline, some plastic Coke bottles, and the powerful firecracker tuna bombs. He filled up each Coke bottle about two inches with gasoline, inserted a tuna bomb in each and screwed the plastic cap down, leaving as much of the wick sticking out as possible. He made six of the bombs and kept them near him. He'd remembered to bring a lighter.

When the rain let up, they opened a few more beers and conversation began until the rain came back and everyone got sleepy.

"We should sleep in shifts tonight," Jack said. "You guys take your naps now. I'll stay awake until I get tired, then I'll wake one of you for your watch."

Jack knew the waters around Mogo Mogo were shallow and the tides ran from minus two feet to plus eighteen feet, according to the phases of the moon, making for extreme currents. Paul had shown him a secret anchorage that was shallow all around but deep inside. Even at low tide there was access to the anchorage and escape, if necessary. Not many people were aware of this phenomenon.

Jack sat back against the cooler, sipping on a beer and enjoying the sound of the rain as it smacked down on his plastic tablecloth. It sounded like a train going by. Jack's thoughts drifted, as they often did, to Tess. He enjoyed her presence, the warmth of her body, her touch, the knowledge that someday, maybe, if he was lucky, she would be his.

The roar of the pelting rain lulled Jack to sleep. He was born in a rainstorm and grew up in the tin-roofed, wooden, screened houses of the Canal Zone. Sleeping in the rain was sheer ecstasy. His eyelids became heavy, and try as he might, he couldn't keep his eyes open. He thought of waking one of the others, but before he could, he was asleep.

A loud crunch, followed by a Spanish curse awakened Jack. It didn't take him long to clear his mind and realize what was going on. A boat had run aground in an effort to sneak up on them. In the big area of water around them, it certainly was no mistake that they meant to rob and kill. Jack quietly woke everyone, including Tess.

"Tess, you sure you know how to handle that shotgun?"

"Did pretty well on the skeet range."

"Okay, crouch down in the doorway. Keep Pomeroy dry, and if you hear me yell out for some back up, you let the bastards have it. Just pump and fire away, got it?"

"Got it."

"It's filled with light bird shot, so it probably won't kill anyone at a distance But these," he slid six shells into her top pockets, "these are buckshot. They will kill. Only use them if we're boarded and you're threatened. I don't want anything to happen to you. I . . . you know I love you. So stay put unless I call out or you have to step over my dead body. Sorry I'm always getting you into this kinda shit."

"I would rather be in this kinda shit as long as I'm here with you. And I love you, too." She kissed his cheek.

"One more thing. Stay low. If they have automatic weapons, bullets will fly. I put a lot of Kevlar and titanium into this boat, but it won't stop everything." He went back into the rain.

"Those cocksuckers'll be off that reef soon," the Dude said, "then what?"

"Here." Jack passed out a bottle bomb to the Dude and Paul. "I've only got one lighter. I'll hold onto it so we know where it is. Each bottle has gas and a tuna bomb in it. The bottle cap is scrunched down on the wick. Just light the wick and throw it. When it blows up, it'll give those pricks a look at what hell is gonna be like."

Everyone spoke in whispers despite the pouring rain.

"Get ready. I'll throw first. It'll light the bastards up, then you all pick your own target. Remember, they might have automatic weapons, so keep low. I have three more bombs, and Tess has Pomeroy and the flare gun. I hope we don't have to kill anyone, but it's them or us."

They waited silently.

The thieves finally manhandled the cayuco off the reef and were in deep water. All hands on the *Arugaduga* strained their ears to hear through the rain. Jack raised up to a crouch. His night vision was excellent. He could see the dark shape of the cayuco approaching with what appeared to be five men in it.

Jack lit the fuse of his bomb below the gunwale of the boat so the pirates couldn't see the light. He held it for a while as the fuse fizzled down. Then he threw the bomb. The sparkling fuse made circles in the dark as the bottle spun end over end.

The tuna bomb shattered the rainy night with an explosion that made the divers cover their ears. A huge ball of flame enveloped the boat, then screams of terror as two flaming figures leaped into the water, leaving three unharmed. One opened up with the unmistakable rapid report of an AK-47. Most of the rounds shrieked over the top of the *Arugaduga*, but a few tore into the water, sending up spouts in front of them. A few more hit the side of the boat, ripping through the fiberglass, Kevlar, and titanium protective hull, but completely lost their punch on exiting into the boat. The Dude was hit by one. He let out a howl and threw his lit bomb directly into the front of the cayuco. It exploded somewhere forward in the boat. All hell broke out again as more flaming figures dove over the side.

The AK-47 was silent for a while, but Tess was into the action now and pumped out a few rounds of birdshot into the tortured, screaming, flaming mess across the water. Her brother lobbed his homemade grenade just as she opened up. Tess hit the deck after three rapid shots. There were more screams after Tess's shots and Paul's exploding bomb, but the guy with the AK-47 was at it again. The weapon chattered its lethal missiles out with nervous inaccuracy.

All this time, the burning enemy boat was drifting toward them. The AK-47 was still in operation, scoring more hits on the *Arugaduga*. A nasty situation was just yards away. Finally, the AK-47 shooter stood up in the burning cayuco. He leveled the weapon at the men of the *Arugaduga* hugging the deck. Everything was lit up from the fire on the cayuco. There was nowhere to hide, and the standing figure on the front of the burning cayuco had an easy bead on the three men. He stood there, illuminated by the flaming boat around him, weapon in hand, looking like the devil's hit man.

A flaming red meteor streaked from the foredeck of the *Arugaduga*. It swished its burning trail straight at the standing killer, hitting him dead center. The AK-47 flew into the air and the shooter flew into the water trying to extinguish the burning flare. Even water wouldn't put it out immediately. Most of it would have to be dug out. Tess had saved the night with her flare pistol.

Three more bombs were thrown in succession. The pirates' cayuco burned throughout the night, drifting past the divers, out to sea. Whoever was in it either took up residence for the night on Mogo Mogo Island and fed the giant green horse flies, the huge blood-sucking mosquitoes, and the persistent gnawing sand fleas, or they became tiger shark bait. The waters around Mogo Mogo were famous for their night-feeding tiger sharks.

"I think we'd better get out of here now," Jack said. "We don't want to have to answer for that burning cayuco. It'll be a different story in the morning, with us as the attackers on those poor, innocent, murdering bastards."

"You have my blessing," Paul said.

"Let's go." Tess climbed into the driver's seat and took the wheel.

"I don't give a shit if I ever see this place again . . . night or day," the Dude said.

They pulled anchor and Tess started one engine. It sounded weak. Jack and Paul stood by her to give her directions out of the anchorage. It was a chilling, slow cruise past the reefs and rocks in the dark, but the tide was high and they had more leeway. They slipped past the inside of Bolanos Island, then around a giant rock in front of the canal to Bayonetta Island. At Bayonetta, they hung a careful, slow left and traveled down another canal. Exiting the canal, Tess started the other engine and put the juice to both. The engines ran roughly all the way to Isla San José.

The rain had flattened the ocean for them and disappeared. All the way to The Monks, off the south end of San José Island, the only disturbance on the flat, dark surface was an occasional ground swell and short flight over a half-submerged tree.

"Fuck!" the Dude yelled.

"It's nothing, it's nothing," Paul said. "Just a tree trunk."

"Puta! I thought they were shooting at us again. Sonsabitches!"

Paul and Jack talked together, off to the side.

"Hey, what's the big secret?" Tess called over to them. "Am I just the driver and not privy to your sacred words?"

"Naw, we were just talking about what to do next," Jack said. They moved closer to her.

"We go home now and someone finds out what went on down here, it won't be long before the Guardia will come sniffing around for us, and it won't matter whether that sonofabitch was shooting cannons at us and twenty AK-47s. Being gringos, we'd be the guilty ones. Also, those engines sound like shit. Probably full of bullets."

"I'll fix the engines," Tess said. "What else you guys have in mind?"

"Well, we were thinking of diving The Monks and coming home with a boatload of fish," Paul said. "Then when we come in and start giving fish away, especially to the Guardia, there won't be that much suspicion."

"That sounds brilliant," Tess said. "And how are you going to explain the forty thousand bullet holes in this floating piece of Swiss cheese?"

"Damn," Jack said. "I'd completely forgotten about that."

"Just a small detail," Tess said to both of them.

"Okay, big smarty pants," Paul said to his sister, "just what the hell would you do?"

"Exactly what you were thinking of doing, except I'd come in at night. If anyone asks why the late return, we had engine problems, and we do because I also strongly suspect that we have a few bullet holes in the engine covers. I'll have to check when we find a calm anchorage."

"Tess, you never cease to amaze me," Jack marveled. "You are absolutely fantastic . . . and not hard on the eyes either."

No one could see her blush in the dark.

CHAPTER FOURTEEN

At first light they pulled in they pulled in behind the jagged face of The Monks. They anchored in a calm spot and Tess got her tools. As she suspected, there were a few bullet holes in the engine covers. The men helped her lift off the heavy engine cowlings and Tess went to work. Luckily nothing was seriously damaged. A hose here, a spark plug there. She quickly repaired the engines, went forward, closed the doors, and emerged in her swimsuit. Even the Dude got an eyeful that started his heart racing. Jack was so aroused, he had to pretend to fix a flipper in front of him.

"Tess, I know you want to dive with us, but I don't want you getting burned, hear?" Jack knew the clear skies, sunlight, and humidity combined would create a fierce sunburn. Even the tanned divers were in danger of severe burns if they were exposed too long this close to the equator. Jack carefully smoothed suntan lotion all over Tess's back.

"Yes, master."

"C'mon, I'm just trying to help you. You wouldn't even be going in the water here if it were up to me. This place has some big things swimming around underneath us."

"Jack . . . look at me." She turned around, grabbed his arm, and looked into his eyes. "I'm a Delsey, and I'm Delsey-trained by that human fish over there, the one and only Paul Delsey."

"It's the best swimmers who drown. Familiarity breeds contempt, and the ocean is very patient."

"Damnit, don't crowd me. I can take care of myself."

Jack stood up, bowed, and made a flourish with his hand. "Mah Hareesh, I am outta here." He backed off bowing, still twirling his hand.

"Well, friends and acquaintances, who's going to drive and who's going to dive?" Jack said to the Dude and Paul.

"I thought Tess was our driver," Paul said.

"She won't listen to me."

Paul walked over to Tess who had put on flippers and mask. She pulled the rubbers back and loaded a speargun. They argued until Paul threw his hands up, turned around, and came back to the other two.

"I'll drive," he said. "I can't talk any sense into that brat. I've gotten old just trying to raise her. Jack, look out for her, will you? She's headstrong and she isn't afraid to try anything. Watch out for her too, Dude, okay? Damn, but I just know she's going to shoot the biggest fish down there."

Paul motored slowly up to the big island jutting out in front of the others. Jack always called it rhinoceros rock because it looked like it had the same armor plate as a rhino. The ocean was calm and clear, but Paul had to constantly be on the alert because the huge ground swells coming in from the ocean could crash over one of those fifty-foot islets. He dropped off the divers far enough out so they weren't affected by the swells.

The water in front of The Monks was shallow compared to other places where they dove. The bottom consisted of massive ledges protruding from the sand. Some of the boulders were as big as a car. This underwater landscape stretched for about a mile out.

The moderate current became slower with the changing tide. Jack saw plenty of fish, but he couldn't concentrate on them. He worried about Tess and stayed as close to her as possible without pissing her off. He watched her swim. Everything about Tess, her movements underwater, the depths she attained, the length of time she stayed down showed she was competent. It also showed her graceful body.

Suddenly something huge came up behind Jack; he turned around slowly. He knew if he made a quick movement, two things could happen. Either the fish would instantly disappear, or a predator shark would sense fear and might become aggressive enough to bite. He relaxed when he saw it was a huge manta ray, a spectacular and harmless creature. It swam up to him, slowly gliding like a giant space voyager.

A speargun clacked and something flashed by the corner of Jack's mask, then Tess streaked by, holding her gun crosswise, ready to release line from her reel, if necessary. Jack swam as hard as he could to catch up to her, but the fish was pulling her too fast. He surfaced and called out to Paul to come and get him. Paul was there in an instant.

"It's Tess. She shot herself an amberjack, I think!" Jack yelled, as he climbed up on the dive platform. "Take me up this way fast." He shook his hand again and again in the direction she was traveling in. "She went by me like a bullet."

Paul sped up to where Jack wanted to get off. "Get her or I'm going in, too!"

Jack had never seen Paul so upset. "I'll get her," he said and slid into the water, leaving his gun behind. He looked from the surface, breathing through his snorkel. The water was clear but there was no sign of Tess. Back in the boat, Paul scanned the surface. Jack made a few deep dives, but no Tess. He dove too deep and stayed too long and had to make a fast ascent for air. As he blasted through the surface, he heard Paul yelling.

"Over there! Over there, Jack! She just came up and disappeared again.

Get her! Go get her, stupid ass!"

Jack swam freestyle on the water's surface, something he would never do when diving. He looked down with his mask and breathed through his snorkel as he swam. Then he saw her. She was down about thirty feet, struggling with the fish as well as for air. She had no more line on her reel, but Jack couldn't tell whether or not she was tangled. He saw the fish, a large amberjack, spinning and swimming erratically with great power. Paul was right. Tess had shot the biggest damn fish around.

Jack dove toward Tess, and when he reached her, he grabbed the gun. He always carried a knife with him after the debacle at Galera. She wasn't tangled, but the stubborn woman was going to drown rather than let go of her gun. Jack yanked back hard with the line in his hand, and the two of them fought the struggling fish as they swam to the surface. Tess started to pass out. Jack grabbed her around the waist with one hand and held onto the gun with the other. Paul had spotted them and was there quickly. He reached down and yanked Tess out of the water and over the side of the boat, where he let her flop onto the deck, choking and coughing. He took the gun that Jack handed him and pulled in a giant amberjack. Jack pulled himself over the side of the boat and immediately went to Tess, who was sobbing between coughs.

"Tess, you had us all terrified. We couldn't find you," Jack said tenderly. He put his hand on her shoulder. "You had me scared—"

Tess slung his hand off. She looked at him with pure anger in her eyes. "Take your damn hands off of me."

"What? What's the matter? What'd I do?"

"You know what you did, you bastard. You interfered with my fish. You went in there and grabbed the line when I was fighting it. I could have gotten it myself. I didn't need any fuckin' help from you. You screwed up the whole damn thing."

Jack was shocked. "Tess, you were out of line. You were thirty feet down. You were out of air, and you had a big amberjack on. What was I supposed to do, watch you drown?"

"I wasn't out of air, and I could have gotten the damn fish by myself!"

"Ahh, I see, you want to have balls like the rest of us guys. Well I'll tell you something, baby, us divers with a pair floating around in our swimsuits welcome help on a fish. We realize it's only a game, but a serious game that could take your life quicker than you could roll a pair of dice. You're a very brave woman. You've saved my life many times, and as far as we're all concerned, you have nothing to prove, you've already done that."

"And you can go straight to hell, Jack Savage. Don't come around me with any of that lovey-dovey shit anymore. You're too old for me anyway." She turned her back to him, walked forward to the small cabin, and slammed the latticed doors behind her.

"Geez, I'm sorry, Jack," Paul said.

"No sweat, I'd rather lose her than have her lost."

Tess stayed in the cabin for most of the afternoon, and when she did come out, she saw a boatload of fish. She could see they were heading for the anchorage behind The Monks. She talked to no one.

"Hey, Paul, do me a favor and take me up to the shore so I can get some of those green Jasper rocks that are rolling around in the gravel on the beach," Jack said. "I'll swim in with this canvas bag. I know a guy back home that can cut and polish them."

"Okay, but then we have to start cleaning fish. It'll be getting dark soon."

"Won't take me long."

Jack searched the gravel beach, which was made up of rocks and boulders, all round-shaped from eons of tumbling in the surf. The beach shimmered green creating a gorgeous yet eerie seascape. Green Jasper was interspersed with gray stones, and the stones above the waterline had dried to a vibrant chartreuse. The rocks were so striking that Jack couldn't stop picking them up, the next one being more spectacular than the last. Eventually his bag was full. He nearly drowned getting them back to the boat.

Jack sat on the side of the boat. There had to be treasure here—bars and coins of silver and gold lying on the bottom right in this bay. There's treasure—I can smell it and I'll be back, Jack thought.

Tess spoke to her brother and the Dude, but not Jack. She heated up some chili she had made at home and told everyone to get paper plates. Paul and the Dude lined up for their serving, but Jack got a cold beer from the cooler and produced a can of sardines from his pack. He sat with his back against the console, picking up sardines with his fingers, throwing them into his mouth.

"Hey, Jack, ain't you gonna get some chili? It's really good, man," the Dude said.

"Nah, been getting too soft eating like that. Think I'll be getting back to the old ways when we used to just bring Vienna sausages, sardines, and beer. I wanna start diving the way we used to. Toughen up a bit." Jack knew Tess heard every word he said. He was also getting drunk, drinking beer on an empty stomach. He had a few more beers, told everyone to be alert and to wake him if there was trouble, slid under his plastic tablecloth, and went to sleep. During the night he somehow tossed off his covering and finished up sleeping in the rain with only his swimsuit for protection.

Jack splashed into the water in the early morning. He needed the shock of cold. Back in the boat, he shook the water off like a dog, wiping his face with his hands. The rest of the crew woke up slowly, except Paul, who was already up, drinking a beer.

"That looks like a good idea," Jack said.

"We're going to have to waste some time if we're going to get in at night," Paul said.

"Hell, we'll dive our way home. Dive a while here, then to Baja De Medio, Niagara rock," Jack said. "There's enough diving from here until shove-off back to Panama to burn any time we need to."

Jack asked Paul and the Dude if they would pull up anchor, and he started up the engines.

"That's my job," Tess said. She put her hands on the wheel.

"I can take care of it just fine. You relax and enjoy the rest of the trip," he said politely. Jack couldn't tell whether the look she gave him was one of shock or anger, and by now he really didn't care.

They dove The Monks, shooting fish before speeding around the southern tip of San José Island, turning north to Niagara Rock. Jack marveled at how calm it was.

"Hey, look at that plane up there." The Dude pointed up in the sky behind them. "Looks like it's gonna dive into the water."

The plane stayed in a dive until it was close to the surface. It leveled off, not ten feet from the water, and headed straight for them.

"Get down, get down! That fucker's not fooling around!" Jack shouted. The plane, a Cessna 172, roared over them, blasting them with its prop wash.

"Sonofabitch!" the Dude yelled, shaking his fist at the rogue aircraft.

"Yeah," Jack nodded, pointing to the aircraft in the distance. "They're coming right back at us."

The plane banked hard, turning toward them again.

"Down again, folks, this kamikaze pilot missed the first time. Why can't I ever have a peaceful trip?" Jack mumbled.

The Cessna buzzed so low it hit the radio antenna, then flew off into the distance and banked toward them.

"Okay, you lousy prick, want to play games, eh?" Jack pursed his lips and squinted his eyes into thin, hard lines. He reached down into his canvas bag of jasper rocks. "Hey, Paul, Dude, come here and get some ammunition." He pulled out two round throwing rocks for himself.

"Let's lay down like he's scaring the shit out of us," Jack said. "Then when the prick buzzes us, let him have it. Lead him a little and let the idiot fly into your rock."

The plane leveled off and started its run. As it was about to race over the boat at an even lower altitude, the three men stood up and hurled their stones. Three throws, three hits. The engine cover behind the propeller took a direct hit that sounded like the lid being slammed down on a garbage can. The passenger-side Plexiglas window made a flat, crackling sound when a green stone shattered it. The last hit was the most devastating—a rock tore into the tail section of the plane and damaged the aileron, making it difficult to steer. The plane turned back toward them.

"These bastards don't know when to quit," the Dude said.

An automatic weapon opened up on them from a shattered window. It stitched the water in white spouts around the boat, before the plane flew off toward Panama.

"Asshole!" the Dude yelled at the plane. "Lousy shot!"

"Maybe not," Jack said, staggering and falling to his knees. "I . . . I . . ." he murmured, trying to get up, then fell again.

Tess ran to him and saw a bullet had gone through his left shoulder.

"It was Diego Pinzon," Jack whispered and passed out.

CHAPTER FIFTEEN

Jack woke to find himself attached to all kinds of tubes with multiple bottles above him. A nurse appeared.

"So, how's the daring diver today?" the nurse asked.

"Not too daring," he said in a quavering voice. "Where am I?"

"In the intensive care unit, Gorgas hospital."

"How'd I get here?"

"Your friends brought you in. You were in bad shape. A friend of mine, you probably know her, Millie Martin, will probably come by to see you soon. You lost a lot of blood. We gave you a refill, though. You're going to be all right in a few days."

"A few days! I can't stay in here for a few days. I've got to get back to work. They'll fire my ass."

"They're not firing anybody's ass, as you so delicately put it. Your boss has been notified, and he said to take your time getting well. Apparently you are too valuable to lose."

"He really said that?"

"Scout's honor," she said, holding up three fingers. "Something else. There's a lovely young lady waiting outside, asking for you. I can't let her in because only family members are allowed, unless you say otherwise."

"Did she have red hair?"

"No, black and curly. Her name is Tess."

"I don't have any family here. Please don't let her in. Send her away, please."

"Okay, but she keeps coming back."

"How long have I been in here?"

"You've been out almost two days."

The next afternoon, Jack heard some talking on the other side of the curtain. It sounded like two nurses, and sure enough, Millie walked around the curtain. Jack could see why the Dude was so crazy about her. She was a really good-looking woman.

"I just wanted to see how you're doing and how you like our hospital food."

"Actually, I'm feeling a lot better, and believe it or not, I like the food." He laughed.

Before Mille left, she said, "Oh, by the way, you have another visitor."

Jack was expecting the Dude, but Tess appeared.

"How are you feeling?"

Jack looked at her stone-faced. "Just fine."

"I was really worried about you. I tried to get in to see you in the ICU when you were there, but they wouldn't let me."

"Thank you for your concern," he said coldly.

"I brought you some magazines and things." She laid a bag down on his table.

"Very considerate. Thank you."

"So how long are you going to be in here?"

"About three more days." He lied. He knew he was going to be discharged the next morning and had a medical statement to his boss for home rest. He didn't want Tess to bother him at home.

"You have a terrible cut across your cheek that you must have gotten when you fell. Couldn't they have sewn it up?"

"Too much time had passed before I got to the hospital and the wound had already begun to heal, but thanks for noticing it and bringing it to my attention."

"Oh, that was thoughtless of me. I didn't mean anything by it. Please forgive me?"

"No sweat, just another mark to show my age." He laughed falsely.

Tess bit on her lip and frowned. "I . . . I wanted to . . . to tell you . . ." She let out a long sigh, struggling with something within her.

"Don't worry, it probably wasn't important. Not wanting to be rude or anything, but I'm getting tired." He lied again. "I need to get some sleep now. Thank you for taking time to come up to see me. It was very kind of you."

"Yes, of course. I guess I'll be seeing you around," she said, her eyes filling with tears. She turned and nearly ran out of the room.

Jack wasn't in much better shape, even if he did hold back the tears.

He was discharged from the hospital the next day. He took a cab home quickly so no one would see him leave. By the time he walked up the stairs to his apartment, he was exhausted. He turned on the air conditioner, changed into shorts and a T-shirt, then flopped into bed. He slept until nighttime and would have slept the whole night through if he hadn't been awakened by heavy knocking at the door. He was groggy and weak, but he got up. It was the Dude. Jack let him in with a sigh and sat down in one of his few chairs. The Dude sat in another after raiding the refrigerator for a cold beer.

"It's really good to see you again," he said. He let out a loud burp. "I'm sorry that I didn't get up to the hospital. A lotta shit's been going on since we got back."

"Like what?"

"Well, no one wanted to tell you about this while you were in the hospital, but Diego's goons broke into your shed and tried to torch your boat. Juan went after them with a machete, and for an old guy, he did a helluva job on them for a while. Chopped the shit outta three of 'em. They say that there were six of the bastards, and they finally took Juan down."

"Did they hurt him?" Jack leaped up from his chair, wincing in pain.

"One of them had a gun."

"What?"

"Gimmee a chance, will ya? Okay, one of 'em had an Uzi an' he shot everything but Juan, mostly your boat. They beat on ol' Juan pretty good. The Guardia at the station by the canal heard all the screaming and shooting. They almost caught them, but they got away. Not before the Guardia put a few bullet holes in them, though. They got the bastards Juan filleted with his machete. That ol' boy has a lotta guts, an' man, can he handle a machete."

"Damnit, is Juan okay?"

"Oh, yeah, 'cept for a few knots on his hard head an' a shiner that no one can see 'cause he's so black." The Dude laughed. "You sure as hell have an excuse for those bullet holes in your boat now."

"Oh, man, I'm not looking forward to patching that fuckin' thing up."

"Everyone can help you. It will be done in no time. Besides, it needs an overhaul anyhow. We can get Tess to fix up the engines."

"Tess ain't fixin' nothing."

"You two still fightin'?"

"That's none of your business," Jack said. "I don't want Tess anywhere near here, and I'll tell you something, she's never, and I mean never, going to set foot on my boat again. You hear?" Jack had a wild look in his eyes.

"Hey, calm down. Don't get pissed at me. I don't give a damn whether she comes or not. Take it easy. Have a beer."

"I'm not supposed to for a few days, but fuck it."

The Dude got two beers from the refrigerator

"I know how to get Diego back," Jack said, putting his beer on the end table.

"He ain't worth it. It'll just be more trouble. The score's more or less even."

"I hate that bastard, and I know just how to put his balls in a grinder."

"Chucha, Jack, y'know he's a dangerous sonofabitch."

"Dangerous or not, I'm gonna piss him off until he's dehydrated."

As Jack's health returned, so did his desire to be with a woman. He had been thinking of Rachel for some time. Now, back to work and wounds healed, he was ready to go. Jack's wounds of the heart would not heal so easily. He missed Tess. He needed her. But he'd heard she was dating a high school typing teacher. Just what Tess needed, Jack thought. He was rather meek, balding, tall, thin, and wore glasses. Not handsome but absolutely devoted to Tess. She would get no arguments or adventure from this suitor. Jack wished them a wonderful wedding and an unhappy marriage.

Jack tried for a week to get Rachel on the phone. Early one morning before work, he made contact.

"Hello?" Rachel's sleepy yawn excited Jack.

"This is a voice from the past."

"Who is this?"

"You don't recognize me?

"Jack? God, it's so good to hear your voice again. Where are you? When can we get together again? I'm completely away from Diego Pinzon now. We no longer see each other."

"Yeah, I'll believe that when I see it," Jack said.

"No, it's true. Walter stood up to him and brought a lot of his well-connected family pressure down on him. Diego had to back off. Walter's off of drugs and alcohol, and he's beginning to act like a real husband to me now. It's wonderful."

"Damn, Rachel, I guess I'd better not be seeing you anymore, if you've finally become an honest-to-goodness bride."

"We started sleeping together again, but sleeping with you is something that I will always make time for."

"Do you want to come over to my apartment for a reunion?"

"When?"

"I know it's quick notice, but how about tonight?"

"I'll be there at eight but I must warn you, even though I have nothing to do with Diego anymore, he hates you. He hates you with a vengeance."

It was eight fifteen when there was a knock at his door. Jack opened it cautiously. Rachel wore a black outfit that set off her flaming red hair. Her low-cut blouse bared the tops of her breasts and enticing cleavage; her face looked radiant.

"It's so good to see you," he said.

She smiled sexily. "I've missed you, too. And this . . ." she said as Jack gently laid her down on his bed and slowly undressed her. She sighed and moaned with pleasure as he kissed and licked his way over her welcoming body. Then she did the same for him until they were both nearly insane with desire.

Their wild sex lasted past exhaustion. Jack finally pulled the covers up over them, and they fell into a deep slumber.

When they woke up, it was past midnight. "I've got to be going. Walter's been on a trip, but he could come home early. I'm a married woman now, you know."

"Yeah," Jack said. "I almost forgot."

The encounter with Rachel sapped Jack's strength, but he went to work anyway. By the time he came home, he was in a good mood, even if a little tired. He ate a meager meal, sat in his easy chair, and promptly fell asleep. He woke up to the sound of someone knocking on the door. His knees almost buckled when he opened the door. There stood Tess. She was absolutely gorgeous, in a white, lacy dress. He hadn't seen her in weeks and his heart jumped erratically.

"Tess. So nice to see you. What's wrong? Can I help you with something?"

"Yes, you can. Let's sit on the couch."

They sat down at a respectable distance from each other.

"So, what's up?" Jack knew by now a conversation with Tess could go a dozen different ways. Hot, cold. Love, hate. He wasn't sure he had the energy for another one of her talks.

Tess looked up and away from Jack's gaze. "I've been wanting to say something to you for a long time."

"Take your time. I've got all night."

"Hell, Jack, I love you. I've always loved you, and I can't love anyone else. I'm so sorry about the way I acted on the boat and the rotten things I said to you. I was a moron to say anything about age. God, you're in better shape and handsomer than anyone I know, and I love that about you. I swear, if you don't love me and marry my sarcastic ass and give me a bunch of children, I'll never marry anyone. I'll become a nun. There, now I've said it. It's off my chest, and now you think I'm a fool."

"A fool? Those are the most wonderful words I've ever heard. I thought you were finished with me. I thought I'd lost you forever. What about your boyfriend?"

"I whiffed him off today. I used him to get you jealous. I felt so sorry for him, but I'm glad he's gone. Please forgive me for my attitude on that last trip, for the things I said to you. I can't even get a good night's sleep thinking about you. I don't know how many times I've said it, but again, I'll tell you I love you."

"I couldn't love you any more than I do. I haven't been able to sleep either. I've been sitting up and thinking about you. You tore my heart out. Nothing was fun anymore. I didn't want to do anything. Now I feel like I'm alive again."

"What about Rachel?"

"What about her?" He still had strong feelings for Rachel, but he didn't want to lose Tess.

"I saw you two together last night."

"Oh. She just came over to tell me that she's doing fine with Walter. He's quit alcohol and drugs, and she's not fooling around with Diego anymore. Walter and his family ran him off."

"Jack, you are one big liar, but I asked for everything I got, so let's forget about everyone else for a while and concentrate on us. No more fighting."

Jack said nothing. He crossed the space on the couch so rapidly that Tess was being kissed almost before she could finish her sentence. He picked her up and carried her to the bedroom.

"Did you screw Rachel here, on this bed, last night?" Tess asked.

"No."

"I'm not going to have sex with you where you just fucked your girlfriend!" She pulled away from him in an effort to get free.

"I changed the sheets. I changed everything. Calm down. You said you weren't going to throw these tantrums anymore. So, what's it gonna be? Are we finally going to be lovers forever, or are you going to leave here in a huff and go home to cry?"

"Put me down," she said.

"If that's what you want," Jack said.

"I can get into the bed myself," Tess said, laughing.

Jack shook his head and laughed too.

They lay in bed the rest of the afternoon and throughout the evening. They talked, made love, talked, made love. Every time they became one, it was as if an angel had come down and slid beneath him in human form. If he was in love with Tess before, he was desperately in love with her now.

Jack and Juan finally repaired all the bullet holes in the *Arugaduga* using Kevlar with fiberglass resin. Tess repaired the two Mercury engines and made sure they had spare parts in a special plastic box. After working most of the day, they went down to the Balboa Yacht Club for a beer.

The club was down at the water's edge. Boats pulled up to the side to have repairs done. Out in front was the anchorage where the yachts were moored. Occasionally, travelers from the sailboats that passed through the canal would walk down the pier to the club.

Jack went to the bar to get a couple of Cerveza Balboas while Tess watched a container ship passing by in the canal, heading out to the Pacific. Before she realized it, a large, burly man sat down across from her.

"Hello, sweetheart," he said in a raspy, drunken voice.

Tess squinted at him. His body odor was offensive, and his hair had the texture of tallow. His beard still had pieces of food on it.

"You look all lonesome, sittin' 'ere. How'ja like to go for a sail?"

"No thanks," she said, looking out to the anchorage and the canal.

"Ah, c'mon," he said, standing up.

He reached across the table and grabbed Tess by the arm. "A little fresh air'll do ya good." He started to yank her up from her chair.

Tess was never one to cry out for help. She immediately grabbed the heavy glass ashtray that was on the table, lifted it high, and planted one of its sharp corners deep into her tallow-haired attacker's head. It didn't kill him or knock him out, but it made him wobble as his eyes crossed. Tess wasted no time in grabbing a beer bottle from someone's table and smashing off the bottom, giving her a jagged weapon.

"Oh, ho, so th' little lady is gonna tear me up, eh?" The bully stood up. He was huge, with hairy arms thick as tree trunks and hairier legs shaped like barrels.

"No, I wouldn't want her to kill you." Jack appeared next to Tess. "That would be a shame to have on your tombstone, 'Here lies a lump of shit killed by a little woman.' Back off, Tess. No, my greasy, offensive rag bagger. I'm going to tear you up."

When it came to fighting, Jack had an uncanny ability to understand the makeup of his opponent and to second guess his moves. He knew what the big man was going to do, and Jack knew how to counter his offense.

"Okay, shit for brains, let's see how you enjoy real pain." The big man hurled himself at Jack in a body block.

Jack had been standing in front of one of the four-inch stanchion poles that held up the yacht club roof. He deftly swung around the pipe and watched his opponent destroy a few of his ribs on the metal pole.

Jack winced. "Oww, that must have hurt like a bitch."

Although Jack was not as big as his adversary, he was a lot quicker. He landed four rapid, mean punches to his face, breaking the brute's nose and possibly the side of his jaw, then jumped to the side in a flash. The man rushed Jack again but was stopped by Jack's powerful uppercut. Jack hit him so hard he almost lifted him off of the ground. It staggered the man, but he didn't go down. Jack went for the stomach with quick, deft punches, but it was like punching a wall. Jack knew his opponent was high on something, probably cocaine. Jack was hit by a powerful punch and sent sliding across the floor. He jumped up quickly. As he was charged again, Jack maneuvered to the side and lashed out with a strong kick to the knee. The big man screamed out in pain, falling to the ground in a heap. He continued to howl while holding his knee. Jack went for him again.

Tess grabbed Jack's arm. "Jack, the poor man is in agony. He isn't moaning for fun or sympathy. I agree he's a prick, but he's hurt, and he needs help, not more punishment."

Someone called the Guardia and some Panama paramedicas arrived with them and carted the big man off on a stretcher. The two paramedics trembled under the immense weight of their cargo.

A bearded bystander caught Jack's attention. "You've done the world an immense favor," he said politely. "You do know who that was, don't you?"

"Never saw him before," Jack said.

"His name is Gary Sweeney, spoiled son of Harold Sweeney. Have you heard of either of them?"

"I think I've heard about the father," Tess said.

"Harold is a billionaire shipper with a fleet that constantly transits the Panama Canal. Gary has had everything he ever wanted, and now it seems he has finally gotten the one thing he never had—a good beating, thanks to you."

"I'd never have had anything to do with the bastard if he hadn't bothered Tess. I don't go around looking for trouble. I know I hurt him."

"Gary's used to always having his way with anything, either by money or force. He's beaten up people in bars and cantinas from Singapore to Panama. He's reportedly raped more than a few women along the way and possibly killed one or two men at different times in bars along his ports of call. Big Daddy always got him off with a lot of money paid to the right people and victims. He is a mean, cruel sonofabitch. I think everybody here owes you a debt of gratitude."

The crowd that had gathered for the action actually cheered Jack.

"Please, please, let's just forget this," Jack said.

Jack took Tess by the hand and left. He had a sick feeling in his stomach, besides having a nasty shiner, a bloody nose, and an opened gash on his cheek. His head felt like a pile driver had pummeled it.

Tess brought him back to his apartment and cleaned him up. Jack had never experienced gentleness and compassion until Tess came into his life. Sex was one thing, but the love she showered on him was overwhelming.

"I can't help wondering why someone like that is such a despicable character."

"Jack, with his kind of money he can be as despicable as he wants."

"Yeah, I know, I know, but I'm talking about what makes someone like that tick. Hell, he's had all the money in the world. Everything his mean little heart desired."

"Because he was born a mean sonofabitch, and I don't trust his ass one bit. What I don't understand is why you always seem to get into it with these kind of people."

Jack chuckled but got serious again. "I'm going to visit him in the hospital."

"Are you crazy?"

"It's something I've got to do."

"Well, if you're going to do it, I'm coming along as backup."

"No, I think you'd better stay here. You know, just in case he acts up."

"You stupid idiot, after all the trouble I've gone through to snag you, you think I'm going to let you put your head on the chopping block alone? No sir, we're going together. And if he flares up, this time he's going to be on the receiving end of a bedpan."

"Now, Tess—"

"Don't you 'now Tess' me. If you have this asshole idea set in that concrete head of yours, we're doing it together."

Tess was by Jack's side like a remora on a shark when they went to see Gary Sweeney at Paitilla Hospital. The brute was recovering from a knee operation that was the result of their grappling match. On the way down the hall, they were surprised to run into Millie.

"Millie, what're you doing here?" Jack asked.

"Didn't Nick tell you I've been working part-time teaching student nurses here? I need the money."

"Gee, I didn't know." He knew Millie made a good salary at Gorgas Hospital in the Canal Zone.

"What're you guys here for?"

"I had a little encounter with a guy named Gary Sweeney and we wanted to see if he was okay."

"So you're the guy who put him in here," she said with a strange look on her face.

"He was bothering Tess, and one thing led to another, an—"

"His room's 302, second from the right," she said and walked away.

"Millie?" Jack called after her. "Did I say or do something wrong?"

Millie turned around and said, "Just wait until you see what you've done to that poor man."

"But Millie, I was only trying to defend Tess and myself. I would have nev—"

She walked down the hallway.

"What the hell was that all about?" Jack asked Tess.

"Beats me. Let's get this damn thing over with."

They found Sweeney's room and walked in cautiously.

"How have they been treating you, Gary?" Jack said in a friendly tone. Tess was silent.

"What th' hell're you doing here?" Gary sat as far up in bed as his painful leg would let him. He had a scowl on his swollen face. One side of his broken jaw was wired up, so he spoke with a closed mouth.

"I just had to come up to see you, that's all."

"You see what you did to me? You were lucky. Damn lucky."

Jack let him boast on.

"Y'know, you're the first guy that ever came close to whipping me," Sweeney said.

"Oh, Jesus, Mary and Joseph!" Tess exclaimed in disbelief.

"What's eating her?"

Jack's hair stood up on the back of his neck, but before he could reply, Tess snapped back.

"Close to whipping you? Who the hell is visiting who in the hospital?"

"Why don't you shut that bitch up?" Gary said.

Tess pulled him away. "He's not worth it," she said. "Let's go."

Millie stopped them on their way out. "Jack Savage, and your last name suits you, I'd have you thrown into the Panama jail if you weren't one of

Nick's best friends. Now you'd better leave this hospital quickly and that means now."

"Damn, Millie's really pissed," Tess said.

"Yeah, some of those nurses take their jobs so seriously. Guess ol' Sweeney really enjoyed our visit, eh?" Jack laughed.

"Oh, Jack, you really made a friend or two there." Tess squeezed his hand.

It had been months since the Dude had been diving, and he was ready to go on a moment's notice. The Dude relished every aspect of diving and would stick by his diving partners come cramp, crisis, or shark. He implored Jack to get his boat fixed up, but Jack said it would be at least another month to get it in running order. The Dude had only helped him once recently while Paul and Polly had helped him every weekend. Unfortunately, the Dude excelled at diving and chaos but not at helping people fix things.

Too much time on land and the Dude got restless. He went diving with some guy he didn't know well and the trip was a complete disaster. No fun, no danger. Just a lot of rain and a leaky boat. He came home cold and tired. He pulled out the bottle of rum he kept in his car. It burned all the way down. By the time he got to Millie's apartment, he was fairly soused. He took out the key she had given him and opened the door. She was in the shower. He could hear the water running so he tiptoed into the bathroom. Before he pulled the curtain back, he heard a cry, then a moan, like someone had fallen and was hurt. He quickly swiped the curtain to the side. He stood as petrified as if he were facing another shark. Millie's back was up against the tile shower wall, and her arms and legs were wrapped around a hairy man who was thrusting himself into her. She was in the throes of an orgasm. The moaning wasn't pain, it was pure pleasure. Neither had noticed his presence until their spasms were almost complete.

"Nick!" Millie cried out.

The Dude turned and walked away, throwing the key on the floor and leaving the door open.

The Dude drove for hours. He was in a state of shock. He didn't know where to go or who to talk to. It was Friday night, and everybody was out having a good time. He hadn't felt this bad since Vietnam. He somehow made it to Jack's house without killing someone, himself, or getting arrested. He scrunched the right side of his car along a concrete post as he pulled into a vacant bay to park. He slid erratically out of the car and went upstairs to Jack's apartment. He knocked on the door, then beat on it, then started yelling for Jack. The door finally opened, and a hand grabbed the Dude by his shirt and yanked him into the darkness of the apartment.

A light went on, and Jack stood over the Dude who had fallen to the floor.

"What the fuck're you doing coming around here screaming and pounding on my door at this time of night?"

"I need help, Jack. Ooh, I'm hurting so bad."

Tess came out of the bedroom wearing a nightgown. The Dude lay on the floor in a drunken, crying jag.

Tess bent down and talked to him soothingly. "What's the matter, Dude? C'mon, let's all sit up here at the table and see what we can do."

She took him by the arm, and he slowly wobbled to his feet. Jack pulled a chair out for him and he sat down. Jack and Tess sat across from him at the card table that doubled as Jack's office and dinner table. The Dude lay his head and arms on the table and continued to sob.

"So what's the problem?" Jack said.

The Dude kept sobbing.

"Great Spearin' Dude, we can't help you if you just keep crying," Tess said gently.

"Millie. It's Millie. She . . ." He put his head down and went into his crying jag again.

"Dude, I'm gonna kick your ass all the way downstairs. If you've got a problem, spit it out, but you're not going to come over here at three in the morning, wake us up, and play guessing games with us between crying."

"Jack, give him a chance to get his act together. I've never seen him like this," Tess said softly, stroking the Dude's arm.

The Dude finally straightened up and rubbed his red eyes. Tess got him some napkins, and he blew his nose as loud as a pelican call. Then he told his story about how he caught Millie with someone else.

"I'm so sorry," Tess said. "Did you see who the guy was?"

"Some big, hairy guy. I didn't really focus that well 'cause I was stunned, but I swear he was someone I seen down at the yacht club a couple'a times. Big beard, kinda pushy."

Jack and Tess looked at each other. "Was he *really* big and hairy?" Jack asked.

"Like an ape."

"Sonofabitch!" Jack slapped the table hard.

"Wassamatta?" The Dude looked at Jack with red, drunken eyes. He barely held his head up above the table.

"I think we know who Millie's companion was," Tess said.

"Who?" The Dude stood up and yelled. "I'll spear him!" He tried to pound on the table but missed and fell to the floor, almost turning the table over and taking the tablecloth with him.

Tess and Jack untangled the Dude from the tablecloth and sat him back in the seat again.

"Y'know th' terriblist thing I ever seen? In Vietnam, we was makin' a sweep an' th' guy next'a me gets his head blowed off . . . an' all over me. That was th' terriblist thing. Y' wanna hear some more? I got lots and lots more."

"No more, Dude," Jack said. "You're not going home tonight. You're sleeping here on the couch."

They put him in the shower, turned on the water, and gave him some soap.

There was a loud thud. Jack and Tess ran into the bathroom to find the Dude asleep on the shower floor, breathing water.

"Hey, how about a little breakfast?" Tess called from around the corner of the kitchen the next morning.

"Aargh!"

"You gotta eat something." Jack poked his head around the corner, next to Tess's. "We've got to bring you back to life, man."

"I just wanna die."

"Die? Did I hear The Great Spearin' Dude say die? Dude, you can always get another woman." Jack suddenly realized he had said the wrong thing—not to the Dude but in front of Tess.

"Uh, Tess, I didn't mean that about you. You know, I was just trying to cheer him up. You know, don't you?" He had the look of a naughty little boy who was trying to worm his way out of being punished.

Tess gave him the fish eye, which turned into a stern look. He made gestures with his hands and shrugged his shoulders. She started laughing.

"Why you," he said, grinning. He chased her around the kitchen and cornered her. They both said "I love you" at the same time when they pulled apart and started laughing again.

"Fuck women," the Dude said quietly, under his breath. "Of course, that's what we're supposed to do."

"What?" Jack said, still laughing in the kitchen with Tess.

"Ah, nothin', just said I'm lookin' for my shoe. How's about a cup'a coffee?"

"That's what we want to hear, oh Great Dude of the Underwater. Sit at the grand table, and it will be served. Anything else?" Tess asked.

"Nahh. Oh, why not. I'll take the works."

After a good breakfast, the Dude was feeling better, but he still felt a stab in his heart about Millie. He couldn't help loving her. The thought of seeing her have sex with another guy turned his stomach. He spaced out until he heard Millie's name being mentioned.

"Dude, listen," Jack said. "Tess and I have figured out why Millie did what she did."

"We know you're still hurting about Millie," Tess said, "but maybe we can explain a few things about the situation."

"Millie wasn't banging him for love. It has something to do with money," Jack said. "She couldn't get it through her head that you could make a living without a steady job. Like it or not, Dude, she went for that bastard's wallet, not his love."

"I think you'd better get used to seeing Millie with Gary Sweeney from now on. He's got money, and she thinks you don't," Tess said.

CHAPTER SIXTEEN

One Saturday morning, Jack was in the kitchen while Tess slept in the bedroom. The phone rang and Jack picked up the receiver.

"Hello, Jack. I've missed you," a sexy female voice said.

"Rachel?"

As soon as he said her name, Tess came in the room. Jack looked over at her with the same look that every man has when he's caught between the devil and the deep blue sea.

"So, how are things going?" he said, trying to be cordial to Rachel while squirming under Tess's angry gaze.

He wanted to explain how even though he loved having sex with her, it was all over between them and he hoped she understood. But he couldn't explain anything to Rachel with Tess staring at him, listening to every word.

"You sound so cold to me. What's the matter? Don't you love me anymore?"

"I'm seeing Tess. Tess Delsey. You remember me talking about her?"

There was silence on the other end of the phone. Finally, Rachel answered. "Congratulations," she said in a strained voice.

"Thank you. Say, how's Walter?"

"We've been doing very well together. After this revelation from you, I guess we'll be doing even better. He's become a very kind man, and he loves me."

"That's wonderful."

"Are you still in love with her?" Tess said as Jack hung up the phone.

"No, I'm not. Nor is she in love with me. It was a wild fling. She was an unhappily married woman. Now they've patched things up."

"Seems like you had a lot of wild flings with her."

"Those were the times you kissed me off and wouldn't answer my phone calls, were going out with other guys, and snubbed me for months. What the hell was I supposed to do, become a hermit or cut my balls off and become a eunuch?"

"Well, the second idea sounds good. Why did she call?"

"I haven't seen Rachel in a dog's age. She called as a friend, that's all."

"Some friend."

"Am I going to be punished the rest of my life for someone I met before you and only saw when you put me out to dry? I love you and you alone. I can't help it if Rachel called me. I've had nothing to do with her since we've been seeing each other. And you've given me some spicy moments with that damned temper of yours since then."

"Okay. Let's just forget about it. The only thing I want you to remember is what I said before. Don't come home with any red hair on you."

"Is that an order?"

"Yes."

"I can handle that," he smiled, grabbing Tess around the waist with one arm and pulling her to him. "Nothing but beautiful black curls from now on."

The Dude still wasn't himself after the incident with Millie and continued to drink too much. Jack and Tess were worried about him. So were Paul and Polly. No one knew what to do until Polly came home one evening and announced, "I think I've got the perfect solution."

"I met someone at Pier Eighteen today," Polly said. "A young woman who had just gotten off an English passenger ship that was docked at the pier started talking to me. She's from Australia but on her way to England to look for work. She's in town for a week, and I think we need to introduce Miss Sandy Colby to the Dude. I'll have a small dinner party for the six of us tomorrow evening. Could be just what the Dude needs." Polly smiled and winked.

Sandy arrived before the Dude. She was dressed in a short, white skirt that showed off her lovely curves and a lacy, pink, low-cut blouse. She wore an opal pendant around her neck. Her blond hair seemed windblown but with an air of control. Her makeup accentuated her natural beauty. She knew how to present herself.

"Hi Sandy, how old are you?" Jack asked, grinning.

"Jack!" Tess playfully punched him on the arm. "You're not supposed to ask a woman her age, especially as soon as she walks in."

"That's all right." Sandy laughed. "What you see is what you get. I'm twenty-five."

"What did you do for a living in Australia?" Tess asked.

"I graduated from The University of Sydney as a regular nurse. I've been nursing for some time now."

"Hey, that's outstanding," Jack said. "You have a boyfriend?"

"Jack!"

"No boyfriend anywhere. Completely unattached," Sandy answered with a big smile.

The Dude was late, giving them time to get to know Sandy. The more they knew, the more they all liked her. She seemed completely at home.

"We're just going to have to keep you here with us in Panama," Polly said.

Finally, the Dude knocked on the door. Polly was pleased to see the Dude was casual but well dressed since she hadn't told him about Sandy yet. She breathed a sigh of relief until he opened his mouth to speak. She closed the door behind her and pushed him out into the hall.

"Dude, how much have you had to drink?"

"Ah, a nip 'r two."

"You smell like a brewery." She leaned forward to inspect him.

"C'mon, Polly, y'know we all drink."

"Promise me you'll behave in there. Okay?"

"Wassa big deal? Y'all 've seen me drink." He staggered.

"Just promise me."

"Okay, okay, I'll behave. Jus' can't see what th' big deal is."

"C'mon, let's go inside," Polly said, opening the door and letting him in.

He muttered to himself. "Still can't see what th' big deal—" He saw Sandy and stopped and stared at her.

"Dude . . . I mean, Nick, this is Sandy Colby, just arrived from Australia." The Dude was speechless. His stare made her blush. "It's a real pleasure to meet you," he blurted out, weaving slightly.

"So you're the famous Great Spearin' Dude everyone is talking about," Sandy said. "I guess sharks don't bother you either?"

"The Dude is the best shark bait I've ever seen," Paul said, laughing along with Jack.

"You guys are terrible," Polly said, but couldn't help laughing either.

"Are you serious? I mean about sharks?" Sandy asked.

They told her all the stupid things the Dude had done on diving trips.

"You crazy Americans are like us Australians, very adventurous. But why is the tiger shark so ferocious, and how do you get away from them when they attack you?"

The Dude poured out all his charm on Sandy with his most winning smile and a liar's glint in his eye. "Tiger sharks will eat anything—boards, birds, rocks, anything—but they always give themselves away when they come up to you."

"What do they do?" Sandy asked, spellbound.

"They growl something fierce like a tiger."

"Really? Then what do you do?"

"I give 'em a board."

Sandy laughed so hard it made everyone else laugh at the Dude's poor attempt at humor. She even accepted the Dude's offer to take her back to the ship.

Polly pulled him aside. "Try to behave yourself on the first date. Don't you dare scare her off."

On the walk back to the ship, Sandy explained she was on her way to England in a week to look for a job.

"A week? Sandy, if I could arrange for you to work in Panama, would you be interested?" The Dude knew Paul and Polly would help Sandy any way they could.

"Well, I don't know," Sandy said, stopping.

"Let's go back to Paul and Polly's house right now and we'll talk about it."

"This is kind of sudden."

"It'll just be a moment and a short talk. I'll get you back to your ship. Don't worry."

"Well . . ."

"C'mon."

They walked back and a surprised Paul answered the door. The Dude explained why they had returned.

"That's a great idea," Polly said. "You could stay here with us until you get settled. What do you think?"

"I'd really have to think about it. It's all so sudden. I mean, I saved for this trip to England, and I'd hate to miss the boat. No pun intended."

"You still have a few days left in port. Let me get a hold of someone I know in Panama. He's very rich, very influential, and he's a good friend of mine." Paul was thinking of Walter. He didn't want to mention his name because he didn't want his sister to commit murder after the party.

"I don't know what to say," Sandy said, smiling and shaking her head. "You're all too kind. I mean, you don't even know me. You just met me. I could be one of those criminals that England sent over to Australia." There was laughter.

"We'll take that chance." Paul said. "C'mon, let's drive down to your ship and get your stuff, then plant you right here with us until we find you a job."

A few days later, Jack took everyone to Taboga Island in his boat to walk through the quaint town, laze on the beach, and swim. They also dove for hundred-year-old bottles thrown over by the forty-niners and others who had crossed the Isthmus of Panama to catch the sailing vessels to California. Jack explained to Sandy it was an English company that sailed most of the vessels. It was called the Pacific Steam Navigation Company based on Morro, the little island connected to Taboga by a sandbar. Taboga was a desirable place to live because there was less disease and no mosquitoes. Back then no one knew mosquitoes carried malaria, yellow fever, dengue fever, and other diseases, they only knew the people in Taboga didn't get sick.

The Spanish had been there too, in the sixteenth and seventeenth centuries. Jack wondered how much gold lay buried somewhere on the island or beneath its waters and when he would have the time to go exploring.

The Dude was a lucky bottle diver. He brought up quite a few exquisite ones, but the best find of all was the white teacup he plucked from the sandy bottom at about fifty feet. It had the steamship company's logo on it with the words Pacific Navigation Steamship Company written in blue. Later, he came up with a matching saucer.

"Dude, you're one lucky sonofabitch," Jack said.

It seemed as though Sandy liked the Dude as much as he liked her. They walked along the beach talking and picking up pieces of sea glass. They found almost every color in the rainbow. The Dude had never noticed the broken shards of glass from smashed bottles and jars before. If a bottle didn't have beer in it, he wasn't interested. But once he knew Sandy used to collect sea glass in Australia, he was ready to pay attention. She explained to him the glass had been tumbled in the surf until it was frosted and had no sharp edges.

"Quite lovely," she said. And the Dude agreed.

Polly smiled, her arm around Paul. "If we can get her a job and a working visa in Panama, I'll bet she stays, and if she stays I'll bet those two become inseparable."

"I'll bet you're right, my little matchmaker," Paul said. He kissed the top of her head.

Around four o'clock they headed back to Balboa, to the Napoli Restaurant for pizza, and then to the Balboa Yacht Club for a few beers with the Zonies.

The three couples descended the wooden staircase to the bar, laughing and looking forward to a good time. There was no room at the bar so they all sat down at one of the large, round, glass-topped tables overlooking the water and the canal.

"Oh, shit, look who's here," Tess said to Jack.

"Who?"

"Your old sparring partner, Sweeney, and his new girlfriend, Gold Digger Millie."

"My, oh, my." Jack smiled and wiggled his fingers at them in a hello gesture.

"Oh, man, catch Millie, she's turning green with jealousy looking at the Dude with Sandy on his arm," Tess said.

"Serves her right."

"Here comes trouble," Tess said, smacking Jack's thigh beneath the table.

Millie was on her way over to them. She took a slug of beer out of the bottle in her hand as she awkwardly approached. She walked up behind the Dude and tapped him on the shoulder. He was in serious conversation with Sandy and didn't respond. She tapped again, harder this time. Slowly the Dude turned around.

"Why, hello, Millie." He greeted her with faked cheerfulness. "How've you been lately?"

"Doin' jus' fine." She slurred her words. "My fiancée's treatin' me real good. Thas' 'im over there." She pointed unsteadily.

The Dude knew Millie was a bomb ready to explode, but like the time he shot the snapper off Galera Island when he knew better, he couldn't resist.

"Yes, we met, remember, in your shower? I can't seem to remember who was humpin' who th' hardest, you were goin' so fast, like a coupl'a bunnies."

"Dude!" Jack said loudly. "That's enough."

The Dude couldn't stop now. "That combination of moans and groans you two let out had any porn movie I ever seen beat all t' hell."

"Dude. Enough," Jack said.

"I tell ya, y' missed your callin'. You and that hairy ape of a boyfriend team up and make a movie like you showed me, lookin' in th' shower at ya, with nothin' on except your birthday suits. Why, you two would be top o' th' list porn stars. Hell, I'd go t' all your movies. You got talent, babe."

Jack knew it was coming. He could see the look in Millie's eyes. Her hand slid up to the neck of the bottle and as quick as a snake bite, the bottle arched up, over, and down on top of the Dude's thick skull with the musical clunk of a bounced coconut. The Dude dropped to the floor, making a one-point landing on his nose right at Jack's feet.

In one unbelievably swift move, Sandy jumped up and delivered a lightning punch to Millie's chin. Millie flew backward, landed on her ass, and slid under a table, out for the night.

When Sweeney saw Millie go down, he charged the table as fast as his healing knee allowed.

"Wait!" Jack shouted. "It's all over."

"What's all over?" Sweeney asked.

"The trouble. Millie beaned my friend, the Dude, the guy lying here on my foot. Then his girlfriend, Sandy, here, clocked your girlfriend, there, who's lying under that table with her shoes sticking out. So, as I said, it's over. The trouble's over. Pull up a chair and have a beer on me. For old time's sake."

Sweeney looked confused. Finally he pulled up a chair and slowly sat down.

"Tess, how about going to the bar and getting our big friend here a beer? Me, too, while you're at it. You are one lovely-looking woman, my dear." He grinned at her.

Tess rose reluctantly, looking at Sweeney. Sandy went over to the Dude and poured a little beer on his face. He sputtered awake.

"I really am dead, ain't I? I'm looking at an angel. Do angels have names?"

Sandy smiled.

"Are mortals allowed t' be kissed by angels? Would'ya kiss me if ya can?"

She kissed him tenderly.

For the first time, Jack and Sweeney had a friendly, if guarded, talk. Jack was amazed at the knowledge Sweeney had about many different things. He had been all over the world and was a self-taught man. Jack asked him about all the trouble he allegedly caused wherever he went. He told Jack he had gotten into some brawls, and some of it was his own fault, but he had never killed or raped anyone. He confessed he was a belligerent, rude, and stupid drunk. Then he apologized to Tess and asked for her forgiveness. She looked at him warily but finally smiled and nodded. All this time, Millie lay under the empty table across from them. Sweeney ignored her as he talked with Jack.

The Balboa Yacht Club soon became crowded. A group of people sat down at the table with the shoes sticking out.

"Hey, you guys know there's a body under this table?" one of the party called out to them.

"Yeah, she's just sleepin' it off," Sweeney said. "Try not to step on her, will ya?"

"Will do," the man said.

"Millie was the one who came onto me," Sweeney said, almost apologetically. "She told me all about the Dude, or Nick, as she called him. Said she didn't care a damn for him. When she made her move for me, in the hospital, I was easy prey. I've always been easy prey for a woman, especially when they're as attractive as Millie."

The Dude shook his head.

"I know Millie's problem. It's money. She's terrified of being without it. It's security that she wants. Well, Dude," he looked across the table at him, "I don't know who she loves, but I know that I love her, and maybe I can trade her security for whatever love she'll give me. I'm sure she loved you, but I aim to try to make her love me."

Jack and Tess were surprised at Sweeney's honesty. Beneath all the bluster was a gentle man, someone who seemed to desperately need friends and someone to love him.

"No hard feelings, Sweeney. I think you'll take good care of her. Just don't run outta money," the Dude said as he massaged his sore head.

Sweeney laughed. "Hey, please call me Gary." He paid for everyone's drinks and stood up. "Well, it's time to get the little lady home. I'm taking Millie back to the States tomorrow, and I'm going to marry her and give her all the security she needs. She quit her job Friday so we could go. Jack, if you ever need any help you can get me at the address or phone numbers on this card, and I really mean it. That goes for all of you, too."

He shook everyone's hand, headed over to the now-vacant table, dragged Millie out, and slung her over his shoulder. She mumbled something incoherent before going back to sleep. Holding onto the back of her legs, with her ass in the air and head hanging down, he walked out of the yacht club. As he passed Jack's party, he waved good-bye.

CHAPTER SEVENTEEN

Thanks to Paul and Walter, Sandy now worked at Paitilla Hospital as a surgical nurse. About a month after she got the job, she moved out of Polly and Paul's apartment and in with the Dude. He adored her.

One evening, he took her to an expensive restaurant. After dinner, he reached into his pocket and clumsily produced a small box. He placed it on the table in front of her.

"What's this?"

"Well, open it," he said expectantly.

Sandy calmly opened the little box, thinking it was some charm or other piece of jewelry. When the top popped open, a clustered pearl ring gave off a dazzling, iridescent glow of every color in the spectrum. Each pearl had a life of its own.

"I dove for those pearls myself." The Dude smiled.

"My God, it's absolutely beautiful! This couldn't be for me?"

"Oh, yes it is. It's my engagement ring to you. Sandy, will you marry me?" The Dude didn't miss a word. He couldn't believe himself. No stuttering. No difficulty speaking. The words came effortlessly.

"You don't know anything about me. We just met."

"I don't care. I love you."

"Oh, Nick," she said, pushing the box and ring back across the table to him. "I'm flattered beyond saying, but I can't marry you."

"But why?"

"Well, because—"

"Because why?"

Sandy took a deep breath, looked to the side, and with pursed lips slowly breathed out. "Because . . . because, there's someone else." She met the Dude's gaze.

The Dude felt dizzy. "Sandy. We been sleepin' together for a coupl'a weeks now. How could y' do that and still have someone else?"

"I don't know what to say. I do love you, more than anyone else."

"Then why th' hell can't y' marry me?" He put the ring back into the box and slid it into his jacket pocket. Then he laughed. He laughed so hard the people around them smiled. "I have to be somewhere in a little while." He laughed again. "Lemme pay the bill, and let's go. If you're still hungry, I'll leave some extra dough for that and some for you t' catch a cab. Probably a lot less ratty than ridin' in my car." He continued to laugh.

"Nick, I'm sorry. I really am."

"Hey, don't feel sorry. Y' got another guy, that's the way things go. Nothin' t' explain t' me. I just wish that you'da let me know long before now. To tell th' truth, that was dirty pool." The Dude stopped laughing. "Hope y' don't let th' other poor bastard know y' been sleepin' with me. Well, I won't be seein' ya around," he said as he stood up from the table.

"Wait, please sit down?"

"Sit down? For what? Y' gonna tell me all th' gory details of you an' Mister Wonderful?" He turned to leave.

"I didn't say that I was engaged to him. I didn't say that I was going to marry him." She raised her voice.

The Dude stopped for a moment and turned around.

"If you still want to come back to my apartment tonight, I'll be sleepin' on th' couch. We'll find a place for you tomorrow."

He slipped away like a startled school of fish.

There was a knock on the Delsey's door late at night. Paul got up from bed to answer it.

"Sandy?"

On hearing Sandy's name, Polly was out of bed in a flash. "What's the matter?" she said.

"It's Nick," Sandy said, tears streaming down her face.

"What'd he do?"

"He asked me to marry him."

"Well?"

"I can't."

"Why not?"

"That's why I'm here, bothering you so late at night. To tell you why." She began crying again.

"I'm going back to bed," Paul said. He disappeared into the bedroom, shutting the door behind him.

"C'mon over to the couch and sit down," Polly said. "Looks like we've got our night cut out for us. Good thing tomorrow's Saturday."

Sandy began with a classic high school romance tale, meeting a boy, Arthur, at fifteen. They went everywhere together, did everything together. He was her first love and they intended to get married. They both went to college, where she became a surgical nurse and Arthur a skilled lab technician. Arthur, in the meantime, developed a taste for alcohol, and every weekend he was out with his macho Australian mates. They drank a lot, played hard, and caroused with women. That's when

Sandy had her few affairs with other men, but still there was no one like Arthur. She stuck with him and discontinued her affairs.

As time went by, Arthur drank more. He became wilder, had more women, and he and Sandy drifted apart. One day while he was out with his friends, Arthur took a dare to dive off a cliff into the ocean. The water was rough and the backwash was white with foam. No one could tell the depth, but Arthur, in a show of he-manship to the girls, flew off the cliff in a swan dive. The water was shallower than he imagined, and he slammed his head into a rock.

"Arthur is a paraplegic now," Sandy said. "He can use his upper body, but his legs are paralyzed for life."

"What about sex and children?"

"Not a problem, but not so easy. I didn't care, though. He grew more and more disappointed with his condition. His personality changed, and I found it harder and harder to take his insults."

"So what did you do to cope?" Polly said.

"That's when I decided to leave for England to give each of us a little time apart."

"Can Arthur still work and support himself?"

"Yes," Sandy said. "He has to do his work from a wheelchair, but he sat at his job anyway, looking through a microscope all day in that sedentary position."

"Do I note a bit of animosity in your story?"

"Well, now that he is incapacitated, he seems to depend upon me for everything. He treats me like a maid."

"Then why do you stay with him?"

"Because I feel responsible."

"Responsible? How could you be responsible for his lack of common sense?"

"We had an argument before he left. I was upset about him being with the crowd he always hung around with. I didn't particularly like them, and I guess I was jealous of all the girls that were with them all the time.

Sometimes he didn't come back for the whole weekend. I could only imagine what went on. Of course we weren't living together, but I was supposed to be his girl."

"If Paul did that to me, I'd kick him out on his ass."

"I told Arthur it was all over between us, and when he yelled back that it was fine by him, I told him that I didn't care if he ever came back. And that's when he dove off the cliff. If I hadn't said that, he wouldn't be handicapped today. It was all my fault." Sandy began to cry again. Polly got her a tissue.

"Were you there when he did it, egging him on?"

"No."

"You said he hung with a macho crowd. Was he a show-off? Did he like the girls to make a big fuss over him? Were there a lot of girls present when he did this act of supreme stupidity? Arthur was a bum, and now that he was hurt, he wanted you, Sandy, to lick his wounds and take care of him . . . until the next new face came along."

Polly didn't spare Sandy's feelings. She told it as it was. Sandy agreed handsome Arthur had no lack of pretty assistants working for him at one of the most prestigious hospitals in Sydney. They didn't seem bothered that he was in a wheelchair. She also said his salary was high, and he wanted for nothing except to walk again.

"When did you decide to leave?" Polly asked.

Sandy dropped her head, as if in shame. "When I walked in on him and a young nurse. They were—"

"Never mind, I get your drift. Does Nick treat you well?"

"Oh, yes."

"Let me tell you a little bit more about him. He seems more Panamanian than American at times. He says he's lucky to be born in Panama from American parents—that makes him a Panamanian citizen and also an American citizen. But his parents were killed in a small plane crash over the Darien jungle so he was orphaned when very young."

Sandy sighed.

"Did he tell you that he earned quite a few medals in Vietnam, saving some of his buddies?"

"No, he didn't. Was he wounded? I've wondered what the scars on his chest and arms were from."

"Yes. He was hit by shrapnel and shot one time."

Sandy grimaced. "Guess there's a lot I don't know about Nick."

"Now the big question. Do you love him?"

There was a moment of silence. Sandy wiped her red eyes with the tissue. She slowly raised her face to look into Polly's eyes and said, "I love Nick more than any man I've ever known and that includes Arthur."

"You have no problem. I think you should write Arthur a letter telling him of your marriage to the Dude, and then continue to live with your husband happily ever after."

Sandy was quiet. Finally, she said, "By God, you're right. I must find Nick. I know he's going to be drinking and won't be home. Where could he be?"

"He'll be at the shed at about seven o'clock in the morning to help the guys get the boat ready for a dive trip. Tess is sure to go. Why don't you? But demand that engagement ring first."

"Polly, thank God for you."

"Here's a blanket. Snuggle up on the couch. I'm gonna go snuggle up with Paul."

Jack, Tess, Paul, and the Dude launched the *Arugaduga* at the boat ramp in Diablo. They second-checked everything and Tess got ready to put the boat into reverse. Suddenly, a car raced around the corner from the old bridge and drove down the ramp. It was Paul's car.

"What th—" Paul blurted out in surprise.

Polly and Sandy got out of the car.

"You've got another passenger," Polly said.

Sandy waded out to the boat with a bag of her things and was helped aboard.

"Wish I could go too, Paul, but I can't handle the seasickness. I'll be on the radio. Be careful." She waved as they backed out, turned around, and headed out.

Everyone was glad to see Sandy except the Dude. He distanced himself from her as much as he could on the boat. It was a bit crowded. Sandy talked to Tess for a while, before turning to the Dude.

"You have something of mine that I want," she said.

"What?" he asked, annoyed.

"You know what it is," she said, pointing to the ring finger of her left hand.

"Oh, that," he said. "I threw it over the seawall on Balboa Avenue last night."

"What a waste," Sandy said, shaking her head. "Now you'll have to buy me one of those cheap plastic ones."

"For what?"

"For our wedding, silly." Sandy smiled. "No respectable girl would think of getting married without an engagement ring."

"Who you gonna marry?"

"You. Now cough up that ring."

Everyone on the boat razzed the Dude until he dug into his duffel bag and came up with the ring box he had left there the night before. Sandy stood erect, holding her left hand out to him. He slowly took the ring out of the box, then stood there, looking at Sandy.

"Why should I?" he said, pouting.

There was another round of razzing and jeering.

"Because if you don't, I'll leave, and both of us will be miserable the rest of our lives. Now put the bloody ring on my finger and make sure it's the right finger," Sandy said loudly.

He slipped the ring on her finger, and they kissed. The Dude walked her to the back corner of the boat, where they could almost be alone.

"What made y' change y'r mind? What about th' other guy?"

"Polly helped me a lot. She made me realize the other guy wasn't worth it. I'll tell you all about it later. Anyway, he couldn't come near matching you for your good looks and wonderful, caring, compassionate soul. I love you, Nick, more than I've ever loved anyone before, and I'd be proud to be your wife."

"Pinch me, I must be dreaming. I've never loved anyone as much as I love you. I promise to be a good husband to you, and you'll never regret marrying me."

"Oh, Nick, I don't intend to regret marrying you. Do you like children?"

"Only in bunches."

"Then that's what we'll have."

Their kiss was one of joy

"You don't get seasick like Polly does, do you?" the Dude asked, rubbing his stomach and making a funny, sick face.

"No I don't." Sandy laughed

It was a classic rainy season morning, calm and hot. The speed of the boat kept everyone cool, but the tropical sun burned down like a torch. Any unprotected part of the body was sunburned in an hour or less. The late morning heat sucked up the water vapor from the ocean by the ton, forming huge cumulus clouds that floated over the blue mountains behind Panama City and hung there. A gentle south wind blew the moisture inland from the Pacific. Later in the day, there would be violent thunderstorms and strong winds as the bursting clouds discharged the water back to earth in torrents.

The plan was to dive Pacheca, Elefante, Monte, Camote and possibly Galera Islands. Galera would have to be hit on the last day, after a sleepover at Ensenada Bay. Surprisingly, Pacheca was hot with fish and they loaded up on corbina and snapper, but it soon turned cold and they were off to Camote.

Paul shot a big snapper right away, then Jack and the Dude each shot one. The three of them had fish on at the same time. Suddenly, out of the blue-green void that separated them from the open ocean, a voracious school of small sharks lunged at them. They attacked like killer bees, ripping at the fish on their spears. The sharks tore, shredded, and bit the snappers to small pieces, leaving only the heads on the ends of the spears. Now the bigger sharks swam up to the heads and swallowed them. The three men jerked and pulled on their spear lines and managed to get the heads out of the shark's mouths. They all burst through the surface and called to the boat. Tess arrived instantly. The divers climbed aboard and pulled in their spears quickly. Tess laughed, but Sandy, being new to this sport, was horrified at what happened.

"Ah, Sandy, this happens once in a while. Sharks gotta eat, too."

"You'll never catch me in that water," she said.

"Hey, y'got nothin' to worry about." The Dude smiled. "They're man-eating sharks."

"Don't listen to those big macho jerks," Tess said. "They were scared shitless, and don't let them tell you otherwise. My brother is pure fish, and when I see him pop out of the water like he did just then, with those other dingalings, I know their *culos* were sucking seawater." Tess laughed hard.

"What's a culo?" Sandy asked.

"An asshole."

"Oh." She laughed. "You know, Tess, I do believe your boyfriend, your brother, and my future husband are as wacky as any Aussies."

CHAPTER EIGHTEEN

Coming around the point of Canas Island, the southern entrance to Bahia Ensenada, Tess spied a white boat at anchor.

"Looks like a pretty big one," she said as Jack slid up behind her and kissed her neck while patting her ass. "Jack! Not in front of everyone," she protested feebly.

He kissed the other side of her neck and squeezed the other cheek. She whirled around, but he caught her and kissed her full on the mouth. She looked at him and shook her head, smiling.

"What am I going to do with you?"

"Oh, you're going to find out tonight, up forward."

"They'll hear us."

"Not if you don't scream and moan."

She made another attempt to clout him, but he grabbed her and kissed her again.

"Hey! Who's driving?" Paul yelled.

Tess recovered the wheel and averted a ground tour of Canas Island.

As they closed the distance on the big white boat, Paul said, "It's Walter's boat, *Rachel Red!*"

Tess looked over at Jack disapprovingly.

Jack could sense her uneasiness. "We'll just go by and say hello. We can't get out of it without looking rude. Walter is a good friend of your brother's. Remember, he got that job for Sandy."

Tess had a sour look on her face and stared straight ahead.

"Listen to me, will ya? C'mon."

"I just don't like it, that's all."

When they pulled up to the side of Walter's boat, Walter was on the starboard rail, waving to them. Standing next to him was Rachel.

"Oh, shit," Tess muttered under her breath. "The fuckin' Red Baroness."

"What'd you say, honey?" Jack asked her.

"Oh, nothing."

Walter insisted they tie up to the stern of his boat and come aboard for drinks. Paul suggested they provide the fish and Walter provide the cook and barbecue pit for a feast. Both motions were easily passed.

"And you said we were just going to be a drive by," Tess said.

"Did you hear me say anything? It was your brother that set the whole thing up. He knows all about the situation."

"Don't badmouth my brother."

"Now you've got me coming and going. You really know how to grab a guy by the short hairs."

"I haven't got the shortest one yet." Tess broke out into laughter.

"Why, you little, conniving wench." He grabbed her from behind and tickled her. She shrieked. Jack stopped and hugged her. Tess closed her eyes and enjoyed the attention.

They tied the *Arugaduga* up to the stern of the *Rachel Red* and climbed aboard the large dive platform and onto the luxurious deck. Walter's captain, a local Panamanian fisherman named Chico, welcomed them. Chico was Walter's right-hand man and had worked for Walter for years. Chico did everything from steering to cleaning. He was also an excellent cook.

The men talked about the usual—bravery, feats of strength, and narrow escapes from death. Finally, the subject of El Gigante came up. Jack relayed to Walter how Diego had tried to shoot them from a small Cessna airplane on the way back from the islands one day. Walter confided that Diego had threatened to abduct Rachel so they were no longer on good terms.

They talked into the night, mostly the men to the men and the women to the women. More than once Tess observed Rachel giving Jack a longing look, but Jack was not looking back. Walter suggested they leave Jack's boat tied up to his and sleep the night in comfort on the *Rachel Red*. Paul and the Dude were all for it, but Jack said nothing. He looked over to Tess, who shrugged.

The three divers remained in their swimsuits, but the women retrieved their bags from the *Arugaduga*, enjoyed the *Rachel Red's* luxurious showers, and got into some comfortable, dry clothes. Jack sat on the port side of the boat and Paul and the Dude perched on the starboard side. Walter and the three women were seated in aluminum deck chairs.

Jack heard a dull thump on the stern of the boat. He had heard a thump like that before, but this time they were sitting in the full lighting of the luxury cruiser and he couldn't see into the darkness. He went into combat mode. Before he could stand up, the transom door blasted open and a man rushed in with an AK-47 in his hands. Two more armed men bounded through the doorway, followed by Diego Pinzon.

"Ah, a little get together." Diego smiled, looking around. "I'm so sorry to crash this party and spoil such a nice evening, but you see, I have some business to attend to, and I need a boat . . . this boat, in particular."

"What do you want with us, Diego? This is piracy!" Walter said.

"I really don't want a damn thing to do with you, Walter, or any of the rest of you, except what's mine. Rachel."

He held out his hand to her, expecting her to get up and come to him.

"Fuck you, Diego," Rachel flipped him the bird, "and your lowlife relatives you brought with you."

"Leave Rachel alone!" Walter stood up.

Diego punched him in the face so hard that Walter flopped to the deck, semi-conscious and moaning. Jack started to get up, but Diego's goons pointed their weapons at him.

"Don't even think about it, Jack Savage. I'll get to you real soon, unless you'd like your bullet now," Diego said.

Rachel was out of her chair and covering Walter with her body to protect him. When she saw his smashed face, she flew into a rage.

Rachel turned, facing Diego, and shouted, "You fucking coward. You were something to me once, a long, long time ago, but now all I see is a filthy murderer. No matter what you do to me you can never, ever make me care for you again."

Diego backhanded her and knocked her down the stairway to the cabins. Jack moved instinctively, but two automatic rifles poked him back to his seat on the side of the boat.

"You really are one fucking coward, aren't you?" Tess said. "Big man, smacking women around."

"Oh, shit," Jack said to himself. "Tess's temper."

"And who the hell are you?" Diego was losing his cool, fast.

"Tess. Tess Delsey."

Diego walked over and grabbed Tess by her thick, curly hair and shook her like a small animal.

Jack was off his seat, streaking toward Diego, when the barrel of a gun laid his face open. He was forced back to his sitting position on the side of the boat. In the meantime, Tess had kicked Diego in the shins and bit his hand.

"Why, you little bitch!" Diego shouted. He released her as fast as one would let go of a rabid dog. "Wait a minute. Yes, yes, now I see. You're

Jack's girl. No one else made a move to help you except Jack. Well, my beauty, we're all in the same boat." He laughed. "We'll have something for you in a little while. Say, were you the one who hit me in the head with a shovel?" Diego's face was crimson red by now.

"No, but I wish I was."

"Hmm." He put his face close to hers, scrutinizing every feature. "Something about you . . ." he said suspiciously. He called for his men to lock the women in a cabin.

"Hey, Chico!" Diego yelled out to the flying bridge on the topside of the boat.

Chico emerged from the dark and climbed down the ladder. He had a broad grin on his face. Diego walked over to him and shook his hand, patting him on the back.

"You did a good job of letting us know where the boat was going to be. We couldn't have done this without you. José, get Chico a gun out of the cayuco," he said to one of his cronies.

Chico's eyes lit up when he held the weapon in his hands.

"Chico, how could you do this to me?" Walter asked through swollen, bloody lips.

"It was easy, Señor Walter. I hate you and your rich things. You have the money, and I don't. I'm nothing to you."

"That's not so. I've always looked out for you. I always paid you fairly. I took care of your medical bills. How many debts have I forgotten that you never paid? Why this?"

"Just shut up!" Chico screamed at Walter.

He walked quickly over to where Walter was sitting and smacked the butt of the rifle across his face. Walter almost toppled out of the deck chair, but held on, gritting his teeth. The side of his face was now a bloody mess.

"That's enough," Diego said.

"Chucha madre, Chico," Jack said in Spanish. "I'll bet Walter fires you for that one. At least, I'll bet he docks your pay for a day or two."

"Can't keep that big mouth shut, can you, Jack Savage?" Diego walked toward him.

Jack had a plan. The three divers had known each other and dove together for so long they could almost read each other's mind. Jack had been making eye contact and signs to the Dude and Paul, and they were waiting for a signal, whatever it was. Jack's antagonizing wisecracks had a purpose, and it was working. All eyes were on Jack, waiting to see how Diego was going to maim him.

"Oh, Diego, using my last name all the time is so formal," he said in a feminine way. "I thought we could have a friendlier relationship, you know, just call me Jack, but I think you're the type that would rather call me Jackie."

Diego charged like an enraged bull. Right before he could lay his hands on him, Jack shifted his torso to the side and came up with a coil of rope. He whipped Diego across the face with it and yelled, "Over!" Then he did a backward summersault into the dark water, disappearing beneath the surface as machine gun shots cracked and peppered the water behind him. No one noticed Paul and the Dude's disappearances.

As Jack dove down into the dark water, he was struck by a round from the machine gun spray. The water had diffused the velocity of the bullet, but it was still lethal enough to rip and tumble across the meaty part of his injured shoulder, leaving an open tear rather than a hole. Jack dove down to the keel of the boat. Without a mask or flippers, he had to swim porpoise-style, feeling his way blindly through the dark water as he searched for the propeller. Barnacles sliced his fingers as he moved. He knew his bleeding shoulder made him a feast for lurking sharks.

When Jack reached the bottom of the boat, he uncoiled the rope and wrapped it around the twin propellers, the rudders, the shafts, and anything else he could find. He tied it off with a simple knot and headed to the side of the boat where Paul and the Dude had exited. Jack swam as far away from the boat as he could underwater. Finally, he had to come up for air, barely breaking the surface like a coconut bobbing in the water. He alternated between the sidestroke and breaststroke toward Canas Island, about a mile away. Machine gun bullets sprayed from the port side of the boat, where he had gone into the water. Jack waited for another volley of shots to ring out. When they did he yelled, "Paul! Dude!"

"Over here!" A cry came out of the blackness. Jack swam in the direction of the voice. Suddenly, multiple shots exploded from the starboard side of the boat. Bullets whizzed overhead and zipped into the water. Everyone submerged. After the shooting stopped, the three divers linked up.

"It's shit city all over again. I swear I seem to live there," Jack said quietly.

"How are we going to free the women, Walter, and Rachel?" Paul asked.

"First, we have to make it to Canas Island alive. Then we can make some plans. The way this current's going may give us some help. Just keep on swimming with it, pointing toward the island. I'm bleeding pretty bad. One of those bastards got me in the shoulder. Be on the lookout for sharks. They'll be coming from downstream. When they get here, I won't hold it against you if you want to split from me. I'm the bait."

"Ah, fuck you." A voice came out of the dark. "We're all in this together."

The three of them swam as fast as possible, trying to keep from splashing and attracting sharks. It was just a matter of time until the swim party spoilers would arrive. Jack chummed the water with his wound.

"Fuck! Somethin' just bumped me!" the Dude cried out.

"I got bumped, too," Paul said. Paul was always cool in a bad situation.

"Kick the bastards, punch 'em, anything to keep 'em away," Jack said loudly, trying to control the fear in his voice.

They were still about a quarter of a mile from the island. The current of the outgoing tide swept them along at about six knots. This, combined with the angle of their swimming, made for a more rapid landfall. More and more sharks rubbed and bumped them. The divers kicked at every slight touch. Finally, they were doing more kicking and punching than swimming. The current had pushed them about fifty yards from the small beach on the island. They were in the middle of what was becoming a feeding frenzy. All their efforts were now directed at fighting the sharks.

"One of the bastards nipped me!" the Dude yelled.

Finally, Jack yelled out, "Just swim for it! Swim for the beach!"

The three divers struck out for the beach, swimming freestyle, in a race for their lives. The tenacious sharks followed them to the sand.

One shark, about eight feet long, actually slid up onto the beach and struggled to get back into the water. The Dude got a big rock and ran over to it as it was ready to slip back in. He smashed the rock down hard on its head, then picked it up and smashed the shark again. The shark wiggled and thrashed about in the surf. Jack and Paul were right behind the Dude with large rocks. They slammed the shark again and again, hitting its nose to damage its sense of direction. Bleeding profusely from its gills, the shark finally worked its way back into the water, swimming erratically. It swam around in circles until the other sharks descended upon it and tore it to shreds.

"That coulda been us," the Dude said.

"We got to check wounds so we can help the others." Jack dropped to his knees on the beach, then fell face down in the sand. He was thoroughly exhausted.

CHAPTER NINETEEN

Diego summoned Chico. "Did you store that extra diesel fuel below before you left?"

"Yes, Señor Pinzon. I put it aboard before we left. Señor Walter didn't know a thing about it. We have more than enough to reach your port in Colombia where you can refuel."

"Fine, fine. You can drop that señor stuff. Just call me Diego. You're my captain now, and you don't have to call Walter señor, either. Just call him sonofabitch or asshole or anything you want."

"Thank you, Señor . . . I mean Diego."

"Good. We're going to make a lot of money, Chico. You stay loyal to me, and you'll have all the money and women you want. But if you ever cross me, I promise to cut you up in such small pieces that even the sharks won't be able to eat you. Do we understand each other?"

"Oh, yes, yes, Diego." Chico looked faint.

"The two women will stay in that cabin together until we get underway. Later, I might let you have the blond one. I want that curly-haired bitch for myself. Rachel will stay in the forward cabin alone, and we'll stuff Walter in the chain locker until we get far enough out to sea to dump him." Diego laughed and slapped Chico on the shoulder. "Start the engines and let's get the hell out of here."

Chico went topside to the steering station on the flying bridge. He started both engines in neutral and hit the switch for the automatic anchor retriever. He pushed the throttles down in the forward position to move ahead to ease the anchor in. There was a loud rumble that came from below, making the controls jump and the whole boat shudder. Thinking he had hit a rock, Chico jammed the controls into reverse. The vibrations and grinding noises worsened. He jammed the throttle down hard forward. The boat nearly jumped out of the water. In sheer panic, Chico left the controls in forward at full speed. There was a slow thumping sound of gnashing gears and a choking squeeze of the propeller shaft, then a terrible whine below the water, and the engines quit. The smell of burning oil was everywhere.

Diego ran up the ladder, yelling, "Chucha madre! You stupid moron, you just fucked up the engines!" He clouted Chico on the side of the head with his open palm and knocked him onto the deck.

Diego tried to start the engines, turning the key back and forth, but they wouldn't start. He shook Chico, dragged him downstairs, and told him to fix the engine problems. Chico told him that he knew nothing about engines, and the only time he had ever been in the engine room was to store the extra diesel fuel for the trip. Diego questioned the three men he brought with him, but none of them knew anything about engines. He went over to the room Walter was locked in and dragged him out on deck, but Walter was as ignorant of engines as everyone else.

"Am I on this boat with a bunch of idiots?"

Diego grabbed a bottle of Ron Cortez, tipped it up to his mouth, and chugged about half of it. He had his men throw Walter back into the chain locker, and they all sat in the veranda below. Everyone drank and tried to make sense out of the situation. Their voices were loud, and their predicament was audible through the thin walls of the cabins.

"We're in luck," Tess said. "They need a diesel mechanic."

"But what good is that going to do us?"

"I'm the best damned diesel mechanic in this whole country," Tess said. "I think I know just what happened."

"What?"

"Well, from what I'm hearing through the walls, when Jack went overboard along with my brother and the Dude, he had a plan." Tess had to whisper so no one outside the cabin would hear her. "Those guys would never abandon us to save their asses, no way. Those engines had to be running perfectly before we came aboard 'cause I didn't hear of any engine problems from Walter or anyone else. Two diesels don't crap out that easily. They're very dependable engines."

"So what did Jack do?" Sandy chewed her nails nervously.

"Jack fouled up the props and the rudders. From the way the boat was jumping around when they tried to start up and go, I'd say Jack did a damn good job of it. I just hope he's okay." Her voice trailed off.

"He'll be all right," Sandy said, taking Tess's hand and patting it. "They'll all be all right."

"Yeah, if they can avoid the sharks. We have to keep our heads and not panic. Those sonsabitches are getting drunk and soon they're going to want women, and we're it."

"But we can't let them," Sandy said.

"Just stand behind me when they come in, and let me do the talking."

Sandy nodded in silence, a look of fear on her face.

The men outside talked louder and louder the more they drank, until they were shouting. The door burst open.

"Understand you guys are looking for a good diesel mechanic," Tess said, as cool as if she were applying for a job.

"What about a diesel mechanic?" Diego asked.

Tess kept Sandy behind her. She maintained her composure and put her hands on her hips. "I said, I understand you are looking for a good diesel mechanic."

"And just where are you going to find one?" Diego laughed.

"You're looking at her." Tess stuck out her jaw.

"You're a woman. What do you know about diesels?" Diego said.

"I went to college. I got a minor in combustion and diesel engines. I can fix any damn engine you show me."

"You talk pretty big, little girl."

"Try me."

"Okay, but you better not be lying."

"I'll fix your engines, and you can be on your drug-dealing way, but anyone lays a hand on Sandy and me, and for that matter, Walter and his wife, I quit. Then you got nothing."

"I'll still have you." He smiled.

"Not if you want your engine fixed."

Diego grabbed her shoulder and squeezed it. She went to her knees in agony.

"You sonofabitch!" she shouted, then turned her head to bite his hand. Diego's hand left her shoulder in a flash. He backhanded her.

"Okay, fix the damn engines, but you better not be stalling for time, thinking your boyfriend's going to save you. They have all fed the sharks by now."

"One more thing."

"What now?"

"I want Sandy to help me."

There was a long silence as Diego looked at her through narrowed eyes.

"All right, but fix those engines, and quick."

When Jack awakened it was daylight. He looked around and saw nothing but the steaming jungle. His arm was sore. Looking down at his shoulder, he noticed a crude bandage of banana leaves wrapped around his arm. He started to get up but fell backward.

"Little weak, huh?" Paul said as he walked up behind him.

"Shit, I feel like a truck hit me. We've got to decide what to do. If we don't get those bastards on that boat out there," he pointed through the trees at the still anchored *Rachel Red,* "they'll rape and kill the women, if they haven't done it already. But we have to wait until dark," Jack said.

"You strong enough?" Paul said.

"I will be."

They all squatted down and watched while Jack drew a plan in the sand.

As darkness fell, the trio of divers walked out of the jungle and down the beach to the water.

"The main thing is to get the boat," Jack said. "Remember, quiet means success. Those bastards are sure to have a guard out back. If everything goes the way it should, they will get a good taste of terror. You guys take care of the boat. I'll take care of the guard."

They slipped into the water and caught the current running toward the boat. Jack's wound bled again, but not as badly as the night before. Adrenaline spurred him on. If he couldn't get Tess back, he thought, the sharks could have him. The Dude was ready for combat and moved through the water effortlessly. Paul swam as smoothly and quietly as a moray eel.

A guard patrolled the deck with an AK-47. The others were below. The *Arugaduga* floated quietly behind the big cruiser. Everything was quiet except for the lapping sound of the small waves smacking against the hull. The three divers knew where to go as they arched quietly into the hull. Each found what he was looking for, then disappeared into the black liquid.

The guard sat on the side of the boat and yawned, the machine gun in his lap. He stood up and looked around as if he heard something. He leaned over the transom on the corner of the dive platform to peer into the open blackness of the water. Suddenly, the silver shaft of a spear hit him below the sternum, ripping through his heart, snapping his spine, and blasting out his back. The shaft protruded out about a foot behind his corpse, then retreated rapidly, back the way it came. The detachable spearpoint lodged sideways over the hole in his back as the attached cable grew taut and pulled downward. The dead man slid over the side and was caught by waiting hands. Jack unscrewed the detachable point's adapter to the shaft, and the cable slid off the spear. Then the body with the spearpoint and cable was let go, and it drifted away with the current.

Paul sliced the rope attaching the *Arugaduga* to the bigger boat. It drifted with the current far from the *Rachel Red* until it was swallowed up by the darkness. The three men slipped into the boat like wet snakes. The whole operation was smooth, silent, and successful.

Tess got the generator going to give the boat lights, which convinced Diego she knew what she was doing. She knew she didn't have much time left. There hadn't been a lot of damage done to the engine, and she couldn't stall forever. She and Sandy had rubbed grease all over themselves to make it look like it was a difficult job.

"What the hell's taking you so long?" Diego asked as he came below to monitor their progress.

Tess and Sandy looked at each other. They knew he was drunk.

"Forgive me, Capitan," Tess said humbly, "but it's going to take a little longer than I thought. You see, something got caught in the propeller, maybe an old net or some driftwood. When your man jammed the throttle down to full ahead, then back and forth, he burned up some parts," she lied. "Lucky that you came along and knew what you were doing and shut the diesel down. Fortunately for all of us, you have a good head on your shoulders and knew what to do. The parts could have been completely burned up, and then I wouldn't be able to fix it. We'll work on it throughout the night, and we should be ready to go tomorrow morning."

Tess bit her lip. She had taken some impressive parts off the engine for show. Actually she could have the whole thing together and humming in about an hour, but that was her secret and leverage.

"What? Tomorrow? What the hell's the matter with it?"

Tess went on with textbook language, explaining to him things about the diesel engine that he didn't understand. She respectfully called him Capitan, was extremely polite, and praised him on his patience and leadership.

"Get the damn thing running, and soon!"

Tess had heard Rachel weeping through the deck.

"Say, Capitan, you men must be hungry. Why don't you get Rachel out of her room and get her to fix some dinner for you guys? Walter said she's a great cook, and she knows where everything is. You're in command here, but I bet you guys could go for a good meal."

Diego laughed as he climbed the stairs to the top deck. He walked down the alleyway to Rachel's room and unlocked the door. She sat on the bed, her eyes red from crying.

"Get to the kitchen and fix us something to eat." He shoved her out into the hallway.

Diego pushed her into the kitchen and sat down. Rachel prepared some plantains and rice and served the food in silence. When she put a plate of food before him, he knocked it onto the floor out of spite.

Suddenly, he heard an engine. It got louder and louder until it was roaring right next to them. The glass window shattered and a silver missile smashed through it, barely missing one of the men. It punched through the bulkhead, then stopped, quivering in the wall. It was a spear shaft with a flat, cut section of a white Clorox bottle on it. "Death Is Coming" was printed on the piece of plastic. Beneath the words was a drawing of a grinning skull.

The sound of the boat faded away into the darkness.

"José! José!" Diego shouted for the guard. He walked through the doorway, shouting, "What the hell's going on out here?"

"José isn't here. Neither is their little boat. Those fucking gringos came back for it. They did something to José. They're coming for us next!"

Diego grabbed the hysterical man by the front of his shirt and shook him like a rag. "Shut up and let me think. I could kill them but I think I'll kill their bitches first." He charged down below to the engine room.

Tess and Sandy had heard the boat pass and the subsequent commotion.

"Get under an engine, Sandy, and squeeze in by the oil pan!"

"No, I won't leave you!"

Diego charged into the engine room and grabbed Tess by the hair. He repeatedly slapped her.

"You fuckin' fool," she said through swollen lips. "If you lay one more finger on me or touch Sandy, I will not finish fixing the engine. It would have been ten minutes more, but now that you've knocked the mechanic and all the parts all over hell and high water, it'll take at least two hours to get this tub moving again. I swear to God, you fuck around with us again, and you'll never get out of here."

"You got a big mouth, little girl. You get that engine running."

"Sandy and I have to steer too."

"What? Why?"

"Because I know these waters, and they're full of rocks and reefs. The boat also has something caught around the propellers and rudders, and if we don't handle the controls gently, just goosing the engines along slowly, they're really going to burn up. If Sandy doesn't help me with the depth sounder to see the rocks and shallow water, and if she doesn't help me with the hard-to-turn steering wheel, when we see the rocks, if something causes me to over-goose these shitty engines, then our ass is grass."

"You don't need Sandy. I'll get one of my men to help you."

"I don't want one of your hairy beasts near me. Maybe you don't understand the situation, but if someone or something causes me to fuck up at the wrong time and we hit a rock, we're going down."

"All right! But I'd better hear those engines running within two hours." He disappeared up the stairs.

After Diego left, Sandy slipped out from beneath the engine and went over to Tess. Tess tried to wipe her face with a dirty rag, but Sandy found some clean tissue from the head they were allowed to use. She wet a few to get the blood off Tess's face. Tears ran down Sandy's face when she looked at her friend. Tess's lip was split and swollen, as were her eyes, but it was Tess who tried to make Sandy stop crying.

Tess didn't shed a tear.

CHAPTER TWENTY

The three divers had pulled around the side of Boyarena Island and anchored. It rained hard. They never took their eyes off the *Rachel Red*. They slept in shifts until they heard the engines fire up. Jack used his small, powerful telescope he stored on the *Arugaduga* to look the boat over.

"Damn! Tess is on the fly bridge driving the boat with Sandy by her side."

He was mobbed for the telescope.

"Well, I'll be a sonofabitch, that's my sister, all right."

The Dude snatched the scope out of Paul's hands. "Thank God, Sandy's all right."

"Don't start your thanking yet," Jack said, taking the telescope back. "We don't know what happened to Walter and Rachel. Diego's men have weapons, and there are still four of them left. I got another bright idea."

Everyone huddled for details on the next play.

The big boat was working but still crippled. The rope had worked its way into the shaft log while still being wrapped around the struts and rudders. Chunks of rope still clung to the propellers, causing a lack of power and a drag. They couldn't attain a speed of more than six knots. None of the men would go into the water to clear the fouled propellers because of their fear of sharks. Diego didn't know that Tess could swim or he would have forced her into the water. He sent the two women topside to steer them out of the channel and into the open sea. Their destination was Galera Island, then the coast of Darien, Panama, and finally, Colombia.

With their AK-47s at the ready, Diego stationed one man aft by the transom and one on either side of the boat along the rails about midship. It began to rain. The men looked nervous. Being the hunters was fine but being the hunted wasn't. One man stood in the rain on the starboard side of the boat as it moved at a slow pace. The engines were in agony as they groaned along, making the boat shudder.

The rain made visibility nonexistent. A humming sound, like a large mosquito, got louder, and it seemed to be heading straight for the man on guard with his AK-47. His eyes were wide with fear as he opened up with his machine gun, spraying the gray rain in front of him. Suddenly the rain parted and a surreal creature with black eyes flew out of it on the bow of a small boat, screaming frightfully and pointing something. There was a loud clack and a silver shaft flew at him in a straight line. It pierced his chest and pinned him to the wall.

The three divers turned sharply and headed out of sight amid the chatter of machine guns and the screeching of bullets overhead. They headed back to Boyarena Island and anchored behind it to wait for the next round of battle.

"Well, that cuts the bastards down to three," Jack said. "Dude, that was a great shot. Wearing your mask was ingenious. It not only kept the rain out of your face, but it scared the shit out of them. Hell, I think he was dead before that spear pinned his worthless ass to the bulkhead."

"I just wanna get Sandy back."

Back on the big boat, Diego was in a rage when he saw his man's body hanging by the spear. He ran up the stairs and jerked both women away from the steering wheel. He jammed the throttle down all the way. The shafts shuddered, then the whole boat rattled and shook. In his state of panic, he pulled the throttles all the way back into reverse and jammed the propellers and shaft. The diesels quit.

Diego stared at Tess long and hard. "I'll kill you before this is over."

"You've gotten me so frightened and shaky, I don't think I can work on the engines. We can sit here while those guys spear you, one by one. They're really good spearfishermen, you know, and they never miss when they have a good target. You sure are a big guy, Capitan Pinzon."

Diego realized Tess was right. "Okay, just get us the hell out of here."

They anchored at the mouth of the bay in deeper water, about seventeen miles from Galera. The women pretended to work on the boat.

The adrenaline ran wild on board the *Arugaduga*. They were playing a dangerous game with spears and bullets. Paul was next to go. The current would help him tremendously, even if it would be a long swim. He slipped into his flippers and stretched the powerful rubbers back on his speargun. He nodded to get underway. He didn't wear a face mask because it would be in the way, and he couldn't see anything anyway.

Jack steered the boat in the direction of the *Rachel Red*. She was ablaze with lights. Jack kept the engine running slowly while the strong current moved them within range of the *Rachel Red*. Then, on Paul's signal, he put it into neutral. Paul slipped into the water and was gone.

Paul drifted and swam for the bow of the big boat. When he reached the anchor rope, he grabbed it and arranged his gear. He took off his flippers and tied them to the anchor line. Next he slung the speargun over his back with a strap he made from a piece of heavy tuna line and pulled himself up the thin anchor rope to the deck. He lay flat on the bow, looking into the open front window, waiting for a target.

A man appeared at the top of the steps, turned, and staggered down the hallway to the stern, his AK-47 cradled in his arms. Paul extended his arm and speargun through the window, feeling his target rather than aiming. He pulled the trigger, and the gun kicked back hard. He knew it was a kill shot without even looking. Paul slipped over the bow and down the rope without a sound. He put on his flippers and headed for the rendezvous with the *Arugaduga* downstream as the guard let out an agonized howl. Diego and his last comrade jumped out of the lounge, where they had been drinking. They found the guard dead, his eyes open in surprise, his mouth agape. The detachable spearhead dropped off the end of the shaft into the widening pool of blood beneath him.

The divers in the *Arugaduga* heard the engines on the *Rachel Red* start up. They watched Diego's man pull up the anchor. Tess and Sandy had climbed the ladder to the fly bridge. The big boat moved ahead slowly. It slipped out of the channel, blowing heavy, black smoke.

"That crazy-assed Tess fucked that engine up on those guys, big time." Paul laughed.

"She's something else," Jack said. "How did she ever get Sandy and herself up on the fly bridge to steer? I can't believe it. Thank God she knows engines. Now we have to create a diversion. We have to make them use up their ammunition before they get to Galera."

The little boat roared out from behind the small island of Boyarena. Jack had to estimate how far an AK-47 round would travel and try to stay out of range. He knew the *Arugaduga* was a well-armored hull. It would be protection from a half-spent bullet but was little protection from a close shot. Jack knew Diego spotted them when there was a burst of automatic fire and bullets zinging over and around them. Spurts of water kicked up in front of them. Two bullets hit the bow and ricocheted into the water.

Jack turned the boat sharply and sped for distance.

"A fuckin' bullet just parted my hair!" the Dude shouted.

"Hang on, Dude! There's more to come!"

The *Arugaduga* continued to dodge the bullets until the Dude was hit in the thigh by an almost spent round. He let out a yelp and hit the deck. The bullet was stuck in his leg and actually plugged the wound, holding back much of the bleeding. He was up immediately.

"Bastards!" He shook his fist at the big boat.

Jack looked through the telescope. "They're trying to pull us in to get better shots at us by messing with Tess and Sandy."

"What're they doin'?" the Dude yelled.

"They can't rape them, steer the boat, and shoot at us at the same time," Jack said. "I got an idea. Get all the fish out of the fish boxes. We're going to do some chumming."

On board the *Rachel Red*, Tess broke free from Diego with one of her vicious bites, taking flesh with it. She jumped on the throttle, jamming it down to full ahead, then reversed it immediately, then back into forward. The engines quit when she secretly hit the kill button that no one else knew about. They were dead in the water, caught in the terrible tidal current of Galera.

Meanwhile, Walter had freed himself from his rope bindings and broken out of the chain locker. He worked his way forward slowly. In the galley, he found a large butcher knife in a lower drawer and searched for Rachel.

Sandy made it down to the stern of the boat and ran into the alleyway for cover. She almost ran into Walter. He grabbed her by the arm, and she screamed.

Walter put his finger up to his lips. Sandy recognized him and calmed down. "Where's Rachel?" he whispered.

"They've locked her in that room over there." She pointed to a door down the hallway.

Walter was not a big man, but he had a reason to be a strong one. He broke the door down with one charge. Rachel was sitting on the bed, terrified. She was trembling like a small animal, and tears streamed down her face.

"Rachel, Rachel," he said as he rushed over to her. He pulled her up into his arms and hugged her tightly.

The last of Diego's men slowly maneuvered down the ladder and onto the stern of the boat. He called out to Sandy. He took a step into the alleyway but was grabbed around the neck. Before he could realize what was happening, a twelve-inch butcher knife pierced his stomach below his ribs and slid up into his heart. He looked at Walter, his eyes wide with surprise. Walter held him firmly with one arm and jammed the knife in his gut, up to the hilt, with his other hand. Diego's last man moved his lips, as if to say something, then all expression left his face as his eyes dimmed and he died. Walter dragged the bloody body over to the side of the boat, where he couldn't be seen from the fly bridge, and slipped it into the water.

The three divers had gone upstream and downstream of the *Rachel Red*, dumping dead fish and chunks of fillets into the water. The sharks arrived. They fought over the fish and the rest of the man's body until it became a feeding frenzy.

"This is it," Jack said and gunned the engines, heading straight for the stern of the big boat.

"What're we doin'?" the Dude asked.

"We're going to board her. Oh shit!" Jack pointed to the fly bridge. "It's Diego with Tess! She looks dead!" He raced up to the stern, bouncing off it. In one swift movement he grabbed his loaded speargun and leaped onto the dive platform of the *Rachel Red*. "Take the boat!" he yelled back to his friends. In one easy leap, he was over the transom and onto the deck. Jack looked into the alleyway and saw Walter. Walter pointed upward.

Jack bounded up the ladder and met Diego at the top. Diego walked toward Jack. He had squeezed Tess around the neck so hard she had passed out. He had Tess's unconscious body under one arm and an AK-47 in his other hand. He pointed the gun at Jack. Jack had his speargun pointed at Diego.

"You don't want to see your little lady get thrown to the sharks, now, do you?" Diego gave a malevolent grin.

"No more than you want this spear sliding through your worthless ass," Jack said.

"I could shoot her now, with just a touch of my little finger."

"And my finger's getting a little touchy on this trigger. Spears are so messy, especially if the quarry isn't killed right away. There must really be a lot of pain in the area I intend to shoot you in. The groin, or maybe up higher, in the stomach. It'll go right through you, snapping your spine on the way out. That must hurt."

"I could shoot you, just as well. I'll just put your lovely lady in front of me." He made a move to do so.

"You do anything but put her on the deck and I swear I'll send this fucking spear through you so fast you won't even realize you're dying."

Diego looked into Jack's eyes. "Let's go below and trade. I give you back your woman, and you give me your small boat. Then we'll part company and never see each other again."

Walter walked out from below, a bloody butcher knife in his hand and his shirt stained crimson. "Hello, Señor Pinzon," Walter said. "Your little friend had a small kitchen accident and fell overboard. Poor man. All those sharks and no one to help him. Ah, well, you won't have to worry about burial costs."

Fear flashed across Diego's face. He knew he was cornered. He put the gun up to Tess's head. "I'll blow her fucking brains out now!" he yelled. "Back off, I'm coming down. Now!"

Jack backed down the ladder but kept the speargun pointed at Diego. Suddenly, Tess wrapped both legs around Diego's leg and cried out, "Jack! How ya doin'?" Tess's grip with her legs made Diego lose his balance.

Diego went into a free fall, and Tess rode him all the way down to the deck for a cushioned landing. His AK-47 flew out of his hands, and it was Rachel who ran out and picked it up. She would have shot him right there if Tess hadn't been in the way. Walter snatched the weapon from her and pulled her to him, back to the alleyway.

Tess leaped up, no longer in Diego's grip, and ran to Jack. She hugged him. He squeezed her hard with one arm, but the other arm held the speargun, pointed at Diego. Diego slowly got up. Even without a weapon he was still a dangerous man. He looked at Jack and smiled. "Well, looks like you have the upper hand now."

"Yeah, kinda does, doesn't it?"

"Hey, you're the winner, Jack. Let's let bygones be bygones. How about letting me buy your boat? I'll give you a good price for it. What say?"

"Now you want to be friends on a first-name basis? My girl looks like she's been mistreated. That really pisses me off. You know, I'd kill anyone who hurt her." He released Tess and gently pushed her away from him.

It was only Diego and Jack on the aft deck, facing each other. Jack put the speargun up and held it out at Diego. "We're going to settle this, man to man."

"Jack! No!" Tess screamed. She tried to grab him, but he pushed her back.

"What do you mean?"

"I mean you and me are going to fight. If you win, you get the little boat and can go. If I win, you'll have been beaten to death and won't need the boat." Jack had the speargun on Diego the whole time. When he finished talking he turned and handed it to Tess. Before he could turn back around, Diego had tackled him. The fight was on. Diego was all over Jack, punching him in the face as he straddled him. Jack rolled over, did a sit out and grabbed one of Diego's long arms. He grasped his hand and bent one of his fingers back until he heard it snap.

Diego let out a howl and stood up, holding his hand in agony. Jack waded into him with rib crunching punches to his sides and stomach area. Diego grabbed Jack around the neck from the side and started choking him, then jumped up and down in an effort to snap his neck. Jack tripped up Diego with his leg, throwing him off balance, sending them both down on the deck. They wrestled, punching each other repeatedly. Jack realized that although Diego was big and tall, he was also a bit awkward. He finally rolled away from Diego's grasp and got to his feet. Jack felt no pain from any of his wounds or his injured shoulder. He was pumped so full of adrenalin from the fight, he was numb to the agony. As Diego got halfway up, Jack nailed him with a swift kick to the face. His neck snapped backward and down he went, flat on his back.

Diego got to his feet slowly. Jack met Diego, free standing this time, fist to fist. Both were bloodied and tired. They stood there, facing each other like two gladiators getting their wind back to go in for the kill. Diego's shirt had been torn partly off in the scuffle. Jack's wound on his shoulder was bleeding again.

Jack's movements were much slower, due to exhaustion, not only from the fight but also from his wound and lack of sleep, food, and water. He attempted another kick at Diego's knee, only to have Diego snare his foot. He finally twisted his leg out of Diego's strong grasp but hit the deck on his back, too tired to get up. Diego managed to get his long, powerful arms around Jack at chest level, face to face to begin a python squeeze. He dragged Jack over to the low railing on the shark-infested side of the boat and bent him over the railing. He released one arm of his constrictor squeeze and put the palm of his hand under Jack's chin, pushing his head back almost to the water. Jack could see shark fins. Jack's neck was breaking and his back was cracking on the railing. The surges of adrenalin in his body were all that kept him from passing out.

Jack pulled his right arm free, crooked it out to the side, and delivered a side slam to Diego's wrist. Diego fell forward. As he did so, Jack twisted out from beneath him. He straightened up and turned toward Diego in time to see him fall over the side. Jack tried to save him by grabbing his ankles. There was a horrible scream, followed by an enormous tug on Diego's legs. A huge ragged fin sliced through the water and as Jack pulled once more on Diego's legs, he realized that was all that was left. Jack immediately dropped the legs into the water and sat down, exhausted. Jack lay down on the deck in a cold sweat. Tess ran over to him and put his head on her lap.

"Oh, Tess, I thought I'd lost you."

"Ha, that's something you'll never have to worry about."

"I couldn't go on if something happened to you."

"Hey, for a little gal, don't I take pretty good care of myself?"

"You certainly do."

"I love you so much," Tess said, tears running down her cheeks. All those tears she had held back during Diego's torturous treatment poured out as she sobbed.

CHAPTER TWENTY-ONE

The afternoon sun had broiled the small, insignificant Pearl Islands and moved to a cooler spot on the horizon. As it journeyed to the edge of the Pacific, it displayed a range of color to remind all that it would be back the next day. Green trees turned violet; drab rocks turned yellow and orange. The ocean became a steel blue streak splashed across the canvas of light, and the sky offered its pinkish red sailor's delight.

Paul smiled at Walter and Rachel and held up a cold beer, saluting them. Walter acknowledged the gesture and waved back while hugging Rachel.

Rachel clung to Walter's arm, new love growing in her heart. He had fought for her fearlessly and had put his life on the line for her.

Walter looked down at her and smiled. "Rachel, we're going on a trip when we get back to Panama City. We're going to the good old USA."

THE CLEAR BLUE LINE 199

"What for?"

"Remember what you told me about you not being able to have children? I talked to my friend, Dr. Morales, before we left. He told me of a new procedure that can help us make a family."

"Really?" Rachel's eyes lit up.

"Yes, we're going to the Mayo Clinic. Then we keep our fingers crossed."

Rachel kissed Walter and whispered something into his ear.

Sandy had her arms tightly wrapped around the Dude's waist. She squeezed him with both joy and relief. She was still trembling from her ordeal.

"It's okay now, Sandy," he said. He stroked her hair, trying to quiet her trembling. Finally, he took her hand and they disappeared into one of the cabins.

Jack and Tess stood on the fly bridge together, breathing in the cool Pacific breeze, as the *Rachel Red* cruised the last leg of the trip. Jack held Tess close to him, his arm around her shoulder. She snuggled up to the warmth of his chest, her arm around his waist. Tess's delightful body, so close, warm, and loving, thrilled Jack.

He reached into his swimsuit, surprised to discover the small bag was still there. He unzipped his pocket and pulled out the little wet pouch.

Tess looked confused. She took the pouch and slowly opened it. Inside was a large, oval pearl of iridescent blue set in a gold ring.

"I hope you don't mind that it's not a diamond." Jack squirmed. "I found it in one of those oysters we dove for that day. Thought it would mean something special to you, with all of our diving and adventures together. I promise you, it's no cheap pearl. The jeweler who made the ring offered me a small fortune for it. He'd never seen a blue one before."

Tess was speechless, and it made Jack uneasy. Suddenly she screamed. "Jaack!" She jumped on him, squeezing him and sobbing. "It's the most perfect, most beautiful thing I have ever seen. I would rather have it than a thousand diamonds. You dove for this once-in-a-lifetime pearl and had it made for me. Oh, God, this is not just a ring. It's a treasure."

"Tess, will you marry me?"

"I wanted to marry you when I was twelve. Yes! Yes! Yes!"

The sun broke through the clouds on the horizon one last time. The two lovers looked through the windswept panorama to the mainland of Panama.

"There it is," Jack said. "I can finally see it. The clear blue line."

"I don't understand. The water's golden."

"Doesn't matter," he said. "It's there in your eyes."

ACKNOWLEDGMENTS

I'd like to thank the following people who made this book possible:

Sandi Constantino-Thompson for reading my manuscript and sending it to my editor.

Lorraine Fico-White, my editor, who did such a splendid job making this book readable. She never quit on me and turned mundane words and sentences into beautiful reading.

Michele Orwin, my publisher, who believed in me, kept the flow of words moving, and stayed interested in the development of the story.

Al Pranke for his expert skills in formatting my painting, drawings, and words into a physical book and for creating a realistic map of Panama.

My wife for all the advice on "how to" and "how not to" write a book. She patiently stopped my screaming and straightened out many a mess that I created.

My fellow divers who I spent so much time exploring the sport of diving with. Without their brave camaraderie, I would have had no story at all.

ABOUT THE AUTHOR

AL SPRAGUE was born in Colon, Panama. After attending college in the United States, he returned to Panama to teach art in high school and college for 15 years. During that time, he painted the landscapes and people of Panama. He was one of the first artists to define the Panamanian culture through art. His most noted works depict native Panamanian women dancing in the traditional costumes of the *pollera* and the *montuna* as well as fisherman who troll the Pacific Ocean for snapper, grouper, and dolphin. Al, an avid fisherman himself, creates fishing lures that are works of art.

Through painting, Al captured the Panama Canal and the men who keep it running. A number of his works were purchased by the Panama Canal Commission and presently hang in the Administration Building of the Canal. Two of his paintings were made into postage stamps of the now defunct Panama Canal Post Office and remain collectors' items. At least four other paintings were recreated as postage stamps for the Republic of Panama.

Al's one-man show of Panama Canal artwork opened the new Museum of the Panama Canal in 2000. Many of his paintings of Panamanian fishermen and native dancers hang in banks and museums throughout the country of Panama and have been purchased as gifts of state for the presidents of Spain, Venezuela, Mexico, Brazil, and the United States.

In addition, his paintings are included in the Presidential Libraries of Jimmy Carter and Ronald Reagan. Al was selected as the official combat artist for "Operation Just Cause" and created a series of paintings which form part of the army art collection in the Pentagon and were featured on CNN.

A consummate storyteller, Al took up fiction writing in his 70s. He is co-author of *The Mahogany Tree (El árbol de caoba)* and author of *Windswept (Vendaval)*. This is his first adult novel.

You can see and purchase Al's art on his website
www.panamaart.com.